PRAISE FOR THE MATERIAL WITNESS MYSTERIES

"Diane Vallere has stitched up an engaging new series."
—Sofie Kelly, *New York Times* bestselling author of the Magical Cats Mysteries

"There's a new material girl in town...[A] resourceful and gutsy sleuth."—Krista Davis, *New York Times* bestselling author of the Domestic Diva Mysteries

"Vallere weaves a tapestry of finely knit characters, luxurious fabrics, and...murder."—Janet Bolin, national bestselling author of the Threadville Mysteries

"With delightfully engaging characters and riveting mystery, it is a series I am looking to see more of!"—*Open Book Society*

"Vallere stitches an intrepid heroine together a nicely layered plot that fits well with the fabric imagery. The secret of the velvet makes for a clever surprise. Fans of Jenn McKinlay's Hat Shop novels may also enjoy this small-town cozy." —*Booklist*

“This entertaining series that began with *Suede to Rest,* continues with yet another fantastic read. In fact, this one may be even better." —*Suspense Magazine*

“Vallere has a good cast of characters as well as a good mystery, but there's always something more.” —*Kittling Books*

“I realized just how much I have come to love these characters when I started the book. It was absolutely fabulous to be spending time with them again.” —*Carstairs Considers*

“This is a well-written whodunit that quickly became a page-turner .... The pacing reached its high point when Poly’s nosiness propelled others to take action and we discover the truth of her sighting. Overall, this was a delightfully entertaining tale.” —*Dru’s Book Musings*

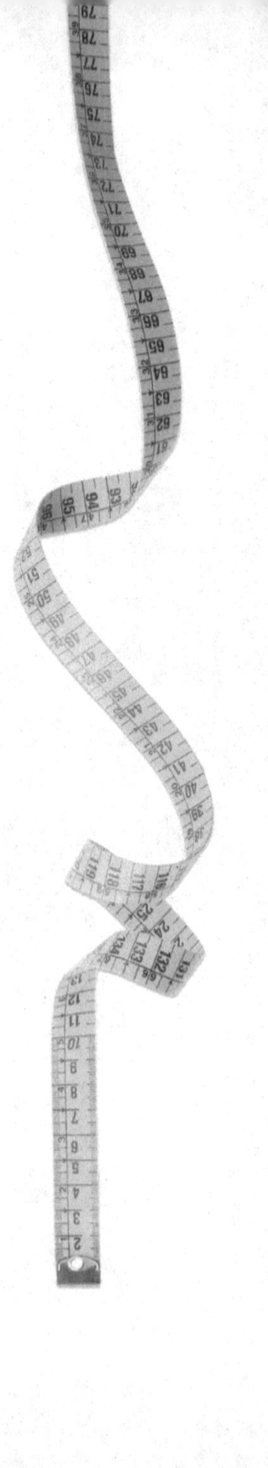

SHEER WINDOW

SHEER WINDOW: A Material Witness Thanksgiving Mystery

Book 4.5 in the Material Witness Mystery Series

A Polyester Press Publication

Print ISBN: 9781954579187

e-ISBN: 9780984965397

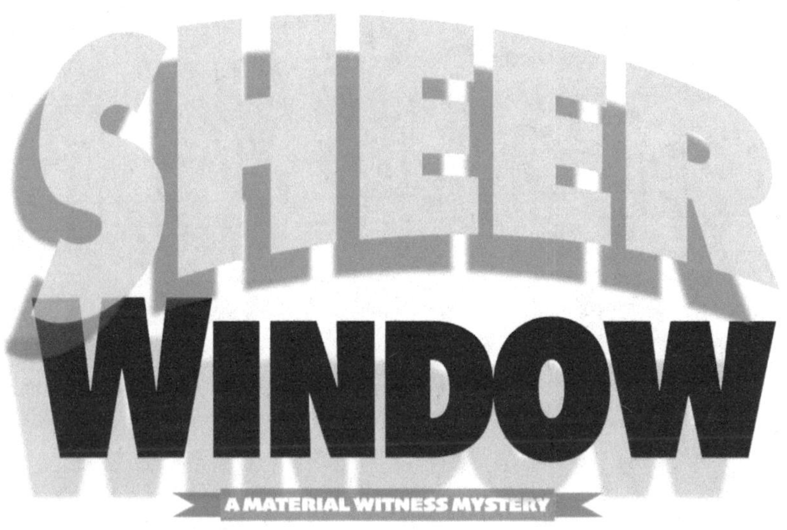

DIANE VALLERE

READING, PENNSYLVANIA

THE MATERIAL WITNESS MYSTERY SERIES

Material Witness Mysteries

Suede to Rest

Crushed Velvet

Silk Stalkings

Tulle Death Do Us Part

Sheer Window

Contesting the Wool

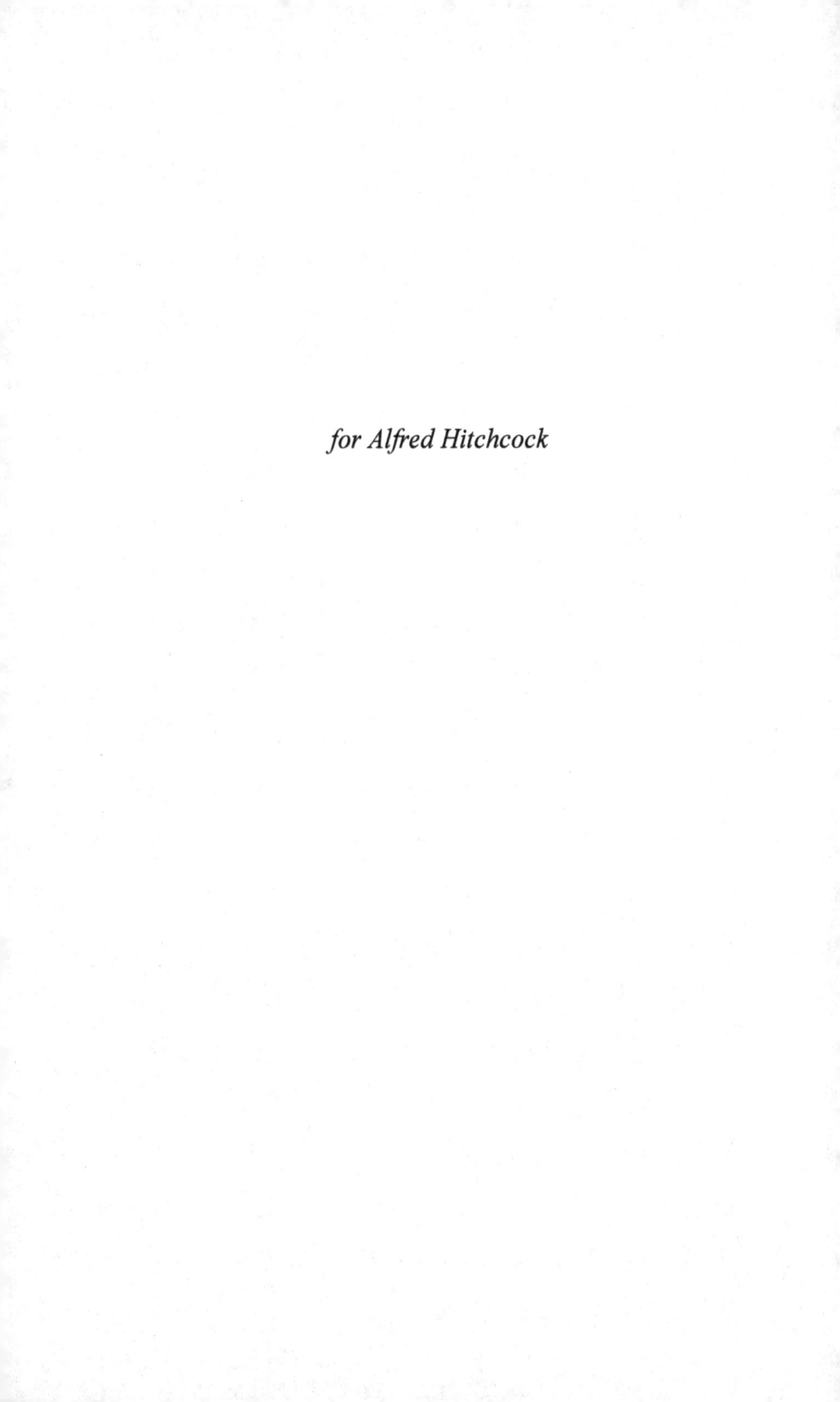

for Alfred Hitchcock

SHEER WINDOW

1

"WHERE'S THE FIRE?" CHARLIE ASKED. SHE STOOD across from me in my fabric store, holding a bag of store-bought buns in one hand and a bicycle pump in the other.

I ignored her dig at me as I rushed around Material Girl, my fabric store, dressed in a black and white tea-length dress that was far too formal for the task at hand. I'd been putting off doing a full inventory of my shop since reopening it this past year, but between ongoing loan payments and new deliveries, I needed more cash and more space. The clearest solution was to sell something off. If I finished inventorying the store before the end of November, I'd be well positioned to find a buyer in December when fabric stores were flush. Come January, everybody in the business would shift to clearance mode and run liquidation sales.

Timing was key, but there was one giant flaw in my thinking, and it was called Thanksgiving.

"Take those buns upstairs. Genevieve's getting my kitchen ready. Duke's there too."

"Duke's already here?" She glanced over her shoulder. "How'd he get up the stairs?"

Duke was a veteran who lost the use of his legs in combat. He owned the Broadside Tavern, the bar across the street. His clientele was a mix of rough customers, who gave the bar a bad name, and local business owners, who understood the importance of supporting each other.

"Big Joe carried him up the stairs early this morning before delivering donuts to the Waverly House. Duke got here before Genevieve. He wants to impress her."

"Considering who she married, the bar for impressing Genevieve is pretty low."

I swatted Charlie. "All of that is behind her. Single life agrees with her. She's a whole different person after coming back from Paris. Relaxed and open to what life brings her way. You might not even recognize her."

Charlie made a *pffft* sound. Charlie didn't like to give in to the notion that people could change because it threatened the very foundation of her whole life. She'd have to forgive a lot of grudges if she ever acknowledged she was wrong.

Charlie stepped away from me and assessed my dress. "Isn't that fancy for inventory?"

"What, this little old thing?" I held up the sides of the ivory chiffon skirt of my dress and twirled. The skirt fanned out. I'm not the most coordinated person in the world, and on my second spin, I lost my balance and knocked into a fixture holding bolts of sheer fabrics. They tumbled like dominoes, but I managed to keep myself upright. "I found it in the back of Aunt Millie's closet. She copied it after the dress Grace Kelly wears in *Rear Window*."

"But you always wear black."

"I wear black for practical reasons. Today is a special occasion, right?"

"According to you, today is just another Thursday."

This time, I made the *pffft* sound.

I left the mess of fabric on the floor and led Charlie to my staircase. I inherited the fabric store and the Victorian apartment above it after my great-uncle Marius went to the great textile store in the sky. The shop had been closed for ten years, and reopening it hadn't been easy. I couldn't remember the last time I pulled the covers over my head and slept for an extra hour. There was always something to do, always some new opportunity to seize or some new bill to pay. People liked to tell me that most businesses failed in the first three years, but I was determined not to be one of them. I'd slow down and sleep when I was dead.

Living above the fabric store was convenient when it

came to my commute home, but the flight of stairs itself was intimidating. By the time I reached the top and entered my apartment, I was a little out of breath. The chiffon of my dress skirt had caught on an exposed nail and left a one-inch tear. I sighed. It would be easy enough to repair, but it was one more thing.

"Hooray!" Genevieve said. She clapped her hands, and flour, the pixie dust of bakers, fluttered into a small cloud. "Inventory is done, and now you can relax and enjoy Thanksgiving." She picked up a tray of orange-clove muffins and extended it toward me.

"Inventory isn't done yet," I said. "I left a bunch of fabrics by the bottom of the stairs. There's a buyer coming to possibly make an offer." I held up my hand, fingers crossed.

"You work too hard," Duke said. He was on the sofa. His wheelchair was empty and pushed to the far corner of the room, abandoned under the branches of a potted tree. My cats, Pins and Needles, were curled up in the center of the seat like yin and yang. Someone had taped a cardboard turkey decoration to the wheel hubs for the occasion. "It's a holiday. Sit down and take a load off."

"But—"

"All work and no play makes Poly—"

"A successful fabric store owner," I said before he could finish the sentence differently.

"It's one day," Genevieve said. She patted the chair

next to her. “All that fabric waited ten years to be inventoried. It will still be there tomorrow.”

It was a losing battle. I smoothed the fabric of my dress and sat on the Queen Anne wingback chair. The upholstery was a print of books in burgundy, chalk, and blue. It was nestled half into an alcove backed with two floor-to-ceiling built-in bookcases, both full of novels and nonfiction accumulated over multiple decades. On the few occasions that I did slow down, I found myself sitting right there, pulling a classic novel from the shelves and imagining which of my relatives read it.

A large window was next to the bookcase, and floor-to-ceiling sheer curtains hung on either side. The news service predicted a storm later today, but I doubted the forecast was accurate. It was a little after nine in the morning, and already, bright sunlight streamed into the apartment, highlighting the colorful pattern of the crocheted throw blanket on the back of the sofa, the texture of the chenille on the cushions, and the wear patches of the Persian rug under the coffee table. It was a homey room, lacking any one design influence, but it reminded me of my family, and that made it perfect.

“Tell me again why you’re working on Thanksgiving?” Duke asked.

“I’ve been open since April, and I’ve made a couple of strategic purchases to fill the shelves. Now that business has evened out, I either need more space, or I need less fabric. I keep getting ideas for the shop, but I can't do anything about them unless I free up some capital too."

"You can't convince me the fabric business runs on a different timetable than the rest of the world," he said. "Today marks the official beginning of the holiday season. Rest, relax with friends and family, and enjoy yourself because starting tomorrow things get real."

I was hoping I'd be able to keep this next part to myself, but there was no avoiding it. "I'm planning to sell off some stock. The silk radzimir, organza, chiffon, and gauze. They take up a lot of space, and there's not much of a need for them in the local fabric market."

"What about wedding dresses? Didn't you make one recently?" Duke asked.

I shook my head. "That didn't go as planned. I think it's better to leave that business to the specialists."

Charlie bit into a muffin and spoke with her mouth full. "Sounds like your business plan is flawed. You don't need money for new fabrics. You need customers to buy the old ones."

"Do I tell you how to run your auto shop?" I asked.

"You don't have to. I've been in the black since the day I opened it."

"When is this appointment?" Genevieve asked. She stood next to Duke. Genevieve owned a tea shop down the street. She'd arrived with the basket of muffins, baked earlier that morning, and an envelope of freshly batched ginger tea, which she brewed in my kitchen. The muffin basket sat on the dining room table. As good as they smelled, we all knew her Thanksgiving meal would be even better, and nobody wanted to ruin our appetites.

"Monday morning," I said. I pulled the curtain back and stared out the window. "But with tomorrow being Black Friday, after today I won't have another chance to get ready for him."

"What kind of person does inventory on Thanksgiving?" Charlie asked.

"A successful fabric store owner," Duke said, parroting me.

I cast a cutting glance at them and looked out the window.

Bonita Avenue was empty. The street was comprised of businesses, bars, restaurants, shops, salons, and one bank—each of them closed for the holiday. Even Lopez Donuts, the most popular spot on the street, was missing the steady stream of customers that usually came and went. Maybe that's why I noticed the person moving around the apartment above Duke's bar.

2

"WHO'S THAT?" I ASKED. I POINTED OUT THE WINDOW. Three of the four people in my living room peered out the window. Genevieve remained in the kitchen, attending our Thanksgiving meal. The apartment smelled like butter and sage and ten extra pounds.

"Is that Tina?" Charlie said, mistakenly thinking I was pointing at the hair salon next to Duke's. "She said she wasn't leaving until noon."

"No," I said. "Above the Broadside Tavern." I leaned closer to my window, as if the six-inch difference would allow me to more easily see inside the usually empty apartment. With an assist from the bright, California sun, I made out a man and a woman moving about the interior of the room. The man wore a purple sweater, and the woman wore a version of my regular daily dress code:

head-to-toe black. The couple faced each other with a buffer of two feet between them. The man held up his finger, pointing at the woman's face. She leaned away. Their body language did not say "happy couple."

"Those are my new tenants," Duke said. Charlie and I turned away from the window and looked at Duke.

"You didn't say anything about lodging tenants," I said.

"Didn't think I had to." He took a bite from a muffin. Duke had a crush on Genevieve and refused to let any of her food go unappreciated, regardless of the feast that would be coming in a few hours. "I finally got the apartment over my bar up to code. Listed it last month and got a tenant the first weekend. Nice couple."

Since moving to San Ladrón, I'd learned that living in a small community meant one thing: we knew each other's business. Initially, I had resisted that, mostly because I was the one being gossiped about. Now that I'd been here long enough for the rest of the community to accept me as one of their own, I was on the receiving end of the gossip.

I shifted my attention to Charlie. "Did you know about this?"

She shook her head. She turned and looked over her shoulder at the kitchen. "Hey, Frenchie. Did you know Duke rented out the apartment over his bar?"

Genevieve appeared with a tray of blueberry buckle.

Duke, ever helpful, arranged two wide round cork coasters on the coffee table. Genevieve set the tray down. Two small creases appeared between her eyebrows. "You rented out your apartment and didn't tell me?"

Duke colored. "Didn't think it was interesting enough to tell."

"Who are they?" Charlie asked.

"I don't think it's appropriate to ask a landlord about his tenants," I said.

Duke said nothing. Despite my words, I waited for him to break his silence and fill us in on the newcomers. He took another bite of his muffin. After he swallowed, he spoke. "I'm new to this whole landlord thing, but I think Poly's right."

"You're not going to tell us anything?" Geneieve asked.

Duke set his muffin down. "Like I said, they're a nice couple. She's some kind of sales rep. Travels a lot. They wanted to live someplace safe. They liked knowing the apartment was owned by a veteran."

"They obviously overlooked the clientele of your bar," Charlie said sarcastically. Duke's Tavern had been known to draw a rough crowd in the past.

"We should invite them over," Genevieve said definitively. "Nobody should be alone on Thanksgiving."

"Are you kidding?" Charlie asked. "Nobody in their

right mind would accept a last-minute invitation to spend a holiday with a room full of strangers."

I turned away from the group and stared out the window again. "Genevieve's right. Come on, Charlie. You're part of the welcome wagon."

Duke sniggered. "There's a first."

"Watch it, Duke," Charlie said, "Next time I might not be so quick to patch your wheelchair tires when you blow one out on a nail."

I grabbed the basket of Genevieve's muffins on my way to the stairs. Charlie followed me. The lack of traffic made it easy to cross Bonita in the middle of the street.

Duke, probably eager to have some alone time with Genevieve, sent us off with his keys. Charlie unlocked the heavy wooden door of the tavern and held it open while I entered. Duke had converted the private dining room of the establishment to an apartment for himself on the main floor, so I'd never before considered that there was a perfectly good, and unoccupied apartment upstairs. I scaled the stairs to the left of the entrance. Raised voices, embroiled in an argument, reached Charlie and me before we got to the landing. I knocked on the door, hoping the interruption would interrupt the fight.

Nobody answered.

"They couldn't have left, could they?" I asked Charlie. "There's no other exit, right?"

Charlie shrugged. "Don't know." She reached forward

and knocked again. "Hello? It's the neighborhood welcome wagon. We have muffins."

"Oh, they're *definitely* not going to answer now." I took the basket from Charlie's hands and set it on a sisal welcome mat that sat in the hallway. "We should leave a note."

"With what? I'm not a stationery store."

"I'll get paper from Duke's bar," I said. "Wait here in case somebody comes to the door. I'll be right back."

I ran down the flight, but I wasn't right back. In my haste, my ankle turned, and I went down in a tumble of white chiffon and curse words, my fall eventually broken by the wall at the bottom of the stairs.

3

AFTER I CAME TO A STOP, I WAITED A MINUTE AND catalogued my various pains. My ankle throbbed something awful and my hip felt tender to the touch. I rolled over and tried to stand but couldn't. I thrust my feet out in front of me and leaned against the wall.

Charlie poked her head around the corner at the top of the stairs. "You okay?"

"I'm not sure." I suspected when I looked, my ankle would be the size of a watermelon. At least it wasn't numb. My stomach churned with nausea, and black spots danced in front of my eyes. My heart thumped against my rib cage.

The biggest difference between Charlie and me was the way we approached emergencies. I raced toward them. She took her time and arrived when she was ready. It was why I was still at the bottom of the stairs in a torn dress with a twisted ankle and a slew of bruises and she took her good old time getting to me.

"Can you stand?" she asked.

"I don't know."

She held out her hands. I grabbed them and attempted to put weight on my foot. Pain tore through me, and I bit down on my tongue to stifle a scream. I looked up at her and shook my head.

"Wait here."

"Not like I can make a break for it."

Charlie ignored my comment and disappeared into the Broadside Tavern while I slowly got on all fours. I put my good foot underneath me and tried to stand while keeping the other foot off the ground. I was pretty sure this was one of the yoga poses I'd never mastered. Charlie returned with an empty bucket. It took another awkward attempt at the yoga pose plus help from Charlie to get me from my spot on the floor into Duke's office. I didn't ask about the bucket until after we'd accomplished the first task.

"Ice," Charlie said. She guided me to the chair in front of Duke's desk and set the bucket under my foot. She got a bag of ice out of one of Duke's refrigerators. She tore the plastic and dumped the ice into the bucket.

This time I howled. “You’re a masochist, you know that?”

She grinned. “I’ve been called worse.”

I gritted my teeth and gripped the arm rests tightly. There was one good thing about all the pain. If my ankle had gone numb, that meant it was broken.

Eventually, my ankle was packed on ice. The next problem was how to get me back home. A collapsed wheelchair rested against the wall under a gun rack with Duke’s prized shotgun. I wouldn’t have minded one of Genevieve’s muffins, but the basket was in the hallway upstairs, still without a note. If nothing else, my spill down the stairs had answered the question of whether or not there were people in the apartment above us. Neither Charlie nor I had been particularly quiet, and any rational person would have opened the door to see what had caused all that clatter.

The presence of a spare wheelchair seemed fortuitous until we discovered one of the tires was flat. Charlie left me in Duke’s office while she went for a bicycle pump from her auto shop a few doors down the street. While I waited for her return, I silently beat myself up for the accident. I’d hoped to finish inventory after everyone left tonight, but a twisted ankle was going to make that near impossible. I wasn’t going to be able to run around the store like I usually did, which meant I would need help. I had a few part-timers, but that meant payroll. Mom and Dad could be called in in an emergency, but that came with questions, lectures, and commentary on my hair, all of which I'd prefer to avoid. I was mostly annoyed that I'd stopped working this morning when I did. If I'd just kept doing inventory until our Thanksgiving meal was ready, I might have finished the task. I sure wouldn't have taken the time to carry a basket of muffins to a mysterious neighbor across the street.

Stupid, stupid, stupid.

I pulled out my phone and called Duke. "It's Poly."

"Everything okay? You've been gone a long time."

"I fell down the stairs and twisted my ankle. I'm in your office with my foot on ice. I was going to borrow your wheelchair but one of the tires is flat. Charlie went to her auto shop for a bicycle pump. Did anybody call or show up?"

"Just Vaughn."

"What's Vaughn doing there?" I felt a frisson of excitement at the unexpected arrival of Vaughn McMichael to our party. We'd been seeing each other off and on until recently, when a wedding in town managed to bring us even closer. I smoothed down the fluffy chiffon of my dress skirt. "He told me he was spending Thanksgiving with his dad."

"He is. They're both here. You want to talk to him?"

That frisson of excitement turned slightly sour. I

didn't answer Duke right away. The answer was complicated.

Vaughn was the son of the investment banker who held the loan that funded my store. About a year ago, when I first inherited the shop, Vaughn and my families had been like the Montagues and Capulets, warring over the property with wildly different ideas of what the abandoned shop should become. One side was invested in the past, in memories and nostalgia. The other side saw an opportunity to get a return on an investment.

At the time, I'd mistakenly believed Vaughn was his father's minion, and I'd treated him accordingly. It turned out that both of us had questions about the history of the fabric store and the fateful event that had motivated my great-uncle to shutter the place. The answers to those questions had affected us in similar ways.

Since then, we'd gotten closer. I never expected to date a rich boy, but nothing about Vaughn said trust-fund baby, and getting to know him was one of the many opportunities life hands us to learn people aren't always what they seem. In his case, that was a good thing.

But Vaughn was other things in addition to my Saturday night companion, and so was his dad. Some of those things affected Charlie. If there was one thing that made Charlie lose her cool, it was being put in an uncomfortable position where she was no longer in control.

I sat, trapped in place, while my carefully planned day got away from me. Vaughn showing up was one thing, but his dad being there was another. The silence stretched as I searched for the right response to Duke's question of whether or not I wanted to talk to Vaughn.

That's when I heard the audible *thud* overhead.

4

"WHAT WAS THAT?" I ASKED, LOOKING UP AT THE ceiling.

"What was what?" Duke asked through the phone.

"I heard something upstairs."

"That's the Estabrooks."

"No, it can't be. They're not home."

"Sure they are—or at least she is. I can see her from here. She's puttering around her kitchen just like Genevieve. I probably should have told the construction crew to install a bigger countertop. Hey, Charlie's on her way back with the pump. You want me to—"

"Thanks, Duke," I said, cutting him off before I had to answer the question. "We'll be back soon."

I hung up and tipped my head back. The Broadside Tavern was rustic. Wood walls, floors, and tables lent the interior a saloon-style vibe, as did wagon wheel light fixtures that hung overhead. Duke had been certain Mrs. Estabrook was in her apartment, and the movement of the light fixture, swaying back and forth from the vibrations of the ceiling, confirmed it. But now, I wasn't as bothered by the fact that neither one of them had answered the door to Charlie, me, and our basket of muffins, but that the thud I heard was loud. Like body-tumbling-down-the-stairs loud.

The door to the Broadside opened, and Charlie entered Duke's office. "Yo," she said. "You actually stayed in the chair. I'm impressed."

I held my finger up to my lips and pointed up. Her eyes flicked up to the ceiling and then back at me. "What?" she asked in her normal voice. "There's nobody there."

I pointed again, this time directly at the chandelier. It swayed, not as much movement as I'd first seen, but enough to see it.

"Vibrations. This is SoCal. Probably an earthquake."

"There was a thump. Like somebody tripped over something and fell."

Charlie glanced at my ankle in the bucket of ice. "You would know how that sounds."

"You're right. I would. I'd also know that the pain of falling is bad enough, and it doesn't help when people make fun of you for being klutzy."

"There are worse things than being a klutz."

At the moment, I begged to differ, but she was right. My accident was a temporary setback, caused largely by me rushing around too fast, trying to squeeze extra time out of every minute. I rubbed my hands over the arms of Duke's wheelchair. My situation was temporary; his was not.

"My point is that someone upstairs could be hurt. They didn't answer the door to us, and I assumed they weren't there, but Duke said he saw Mrs. Estabrook in her kitchen. Notice how quiet it is?"

We both stood still and listened for sounds overhead. There were none.

Charlie leaned forward and tore the top sheet off the notepad Duke kept by his phone. She pulled a pen out of a coffee cup with a logo for Jitterbug, the local coffee shop, and poised the pen over the paper. At my stare, she said, "What? You're the one who wanted to leave a note."

"If she's unconscious on the floor, I don't think a note is going to help."

"Fine. I'll go check on her." She left me alone again. Footsteps went up the stairs. A few seconds later, they thumped back down. "No answer. What now?"

I tapped my front teeth while I followed my concerns through. "If Mrs. Estabrook was alone in her kitchen and fell, she could be hurt. She could be in worse condition than I am. And if she was cooking, her oven might be on, which means there's a possibility of a gas leak or something burning if left unattended."

"So what? You just said she didn't answer the door when we knocked the first time. You think the welcome wagon should break down the door?"

"I think we should call the cops."

"Heck no."

"Hear me out. We came over here innocently, to deliver a basket of muffins to a new neighbor. We overheard voices, but nobody answered the door. I fell down the stairs and nobody came out to check on the noise. Then when I was downstairs, I heard a *thud*, and now it's quiet. That is enough to warrant a visit from Clark."

"You can call him if you want, but I don't plan to be here when you do."

"You're abandoning me?"

"Self-preservation. Me and Clark don't mix."

"The list of people you avoid these days keeps on getting longer."

"My list is short." She ticked her fingers. "Clark and people named McMichael."

"What's wrong with people named McMichael?" Vaughn asked, surprising us both with his entry into the Broadside Tavern.

Despite what Charlie had said, she had nothing against Vaughn. "'Sup, bro?" she said.

"Duke said you needed help." He took in my foot in the white bucket of ice, and his forehead creased in concern. "Do you need a doctor?"

"I need for you both to stop fussing over my ankle and listen to me. Something happened in the apartment above the bar, and we need to call Clark and have him investigate."

"Duke found a tenant?" Vaughn asked, looking up at the ceiling. The wagon wheel chandelier had stopped moving.

"You knew he was going to rent the place out?" I asked. "You never said anything."

"I helped him with the paperwork to designate it for living space, but I didn't know somebody moved in."

"Duke finally got it up to code, and he rented it out to a couple: Mr. and Mrs. Estabrook. She's a regional sales rep and travels a lot. We took them a basket of Genevieve's muffins as a welcome-to-the-neighborhood gesture, but nobody answered the door."

"I'd hate to see the crib sheet you made on me when we first met," Vaughn said. He bent down and kissed me to let me know he was joking. "What's Clark got to do with anything?"

"Poly thinks something nefarious happened to Mrs. Estabrook." Charlie waggled her eyebrows up and down.

Vaughn found himself in the unenviable position of having to weigh Charlie's word against mine. He was nothing if not diplomatic, which went a long way toward ensuring his ongoing popularity in San Ladrón despite what a lot of people thought about his dad.

At the thought of his dad, I remembered the surprise Charlie would walk into when she returned to my place. Clark was the lesser of two evils. If Charlie returned to my place and found Vic McMichael there, she'd turn right around and eat Thanksgiving dinner on a hubcap in her auto shop.

"Humor me," I said. "Call Clark and have him check it out."

5

THE SHERIFF'S MOBILE UNIT WAS LESS THAN A MILE FROM the Broadside Tavern, and Sheriff Clark arrived quickly. San Ladrón was a small town and until recently, largely untouched by crime. Clark was a one-man law enforcement presence, though the city of Los Angeles occasionally flexed a rotation of deputy sheriffs to us when needed.

Thanksgiving was not a high-crime day in San Ladrón, and Clark had planned to spend his shift in the sheriff's office with a pot of coffee and a crossword puzzle. At four, he'd turn on the game. At six, he'd trade coffee for beer. At eight, barring any interference, he'd likely fall asleep on the sofa inside the mobile unit where he'd wake tomorrow with a stiff neck and Genevieve out front with a Tupperware of leftovers.

I shared my concerns about the new tenant in Duke's apartment with Clark, leaving out suspicions of anything other than accidental mishaps. "It's been quiet since I heard the thud," I said. "If Mrs. Estabrook fell, she didn't get up."

Clark glanced at the ceiling. "I didn't know Duke rented the place."

"That does seem to be the surprise of the day," I said. I glanced at Vaughn. "Can't you go up there and check it out?"

"You sure she didn't leave?"

"Duke said he saw her in her kitchen from my place."

As soon as I said it, I regretted it. When Genevieve first approached me with the idea of hosting Thanksgiving dinner, it was for a small group of orphans who had no other plans. Charlie, Duke, Genevieve, and me. A tiny part of me thought it might be Genevieve's way of orchestrating a day with Duke, and I wanted to support her in her attempts to rejoin the dating public. Now our party had grown by two: Vaughn and his dad, though Clark had no way of knowing their presence wasn't part of the plan (a plan I had yet to tell Charlie). "I can bring you leftovers later, if you want."

Charlie scowled at me for being nice to the enemy.

Sheriff Clark ignored Charlie's reaction and nodded. "I'll knock on the door, but if nobody answers, there's nothing else I can do."

"That's something."

He addressed Vaughn. "If you wait here, I'll help you get Poly back to her place when I'm done."

"What?" Charlie and I asked in unison.

"Between that flat tire and the flight of steps inside your place, you're not going to make it to your own Thanksgiving meal without some help."

I didn't love the idea of needing Vaughn and Clark's help, but Charlie liked the idea even less. "We can eat downstairs in the fabric store."

"No, we can't," I said. "Maybe you don't mind your auto shop smelling like food, but fabric soaks up smells, and my business model doesn't include scratch-and-sniff material. We're eating upstairs."

The sheriff nodded, silently agreeing that my idea was best, which didn't help his case with Charlie.

He left us in the Broadside Tavern and ascended the stairs. *Thump, thump, thump, thump.* If I'd had my way, I would have demanded silence while he pounded on the door, but I was overruled. Against my protests, Vaughn lifted me out of the wheelchair and set me on a barstool. Charlie used the bicycle pump deftly and attempted to inflate the tire. It soon became apparent that the tire wasn't just flat, the rubber was rotted through, and any efforts short of replacing it would be futile.

Clark returned. "What you heard was nothing more than a kitchen accident. Mrs. Estabrook dropped a Dutch oven on her foot. Gravy everywhere. Left a big mess on the rug."

"What about the voices we heard?" I asked. "It sounded like people arguing."

"Probably her TV. It was on mute when she answered the door."

"Did you see Mr. Estabrook?"

"She said he was taking a nap. Sorry to disappoint you, Poly, but there's nothing suspicious in that apartment."

I wasn't as willing as Clark to write off my suspicions, but I also wasn't in a position to check things out on my own.

Getting me to my apartment was an embarrassing production. At five foot nine, I'm taller than most women, which creates certain inconveniences. After a little discussion, I agreed to sit in Duke's wheelchair while Vaughn and Clark each took a side. Charlie dumped the ice on a patch of grass by the sidewalk and followed with the empty bucket.

Vaughn stepped around the stack of fabric bolts and carried me up the stairs, and Clark followed with Duke's chair. I was hyperaware of the sensation of Vaughn's arm on the back of my legs, and wished I'd worn black trousers and a turtleneck instead of the fluffy *Rear Window* dress, but there was nothing I could do about that now. Clark propped the wheelchair against a wall—it was no use to anybody with that flat tire—and went back to the sheriff's mobile unit with half of Genevieve's blueberry buckle in a Tupperware container under his arm.

The apartment smelled divine. In addition to the sage and butter scents from earlier, a tray of freshly baked cranberry bars sat next to a carafe of mulled wine on the coffee table. Duke was in the kitchen with Genevieve, peeling potatoes at the table while she cooked.

"Use my wheelchair," Duke said. "Gen's keeping me busy in here."

"Duke makes a good sous-chef," Genevieve joked.

With everything else that had happened that morning, it was nice to see Duke and Genevieve maintain their innocent flirtation. It had been less than a year since Genevieve became a widow, and enough troubling information about her husband had left her shellshocked. She was still coming into her own after the fallout. She was learning to be less tentative in life, but in the kitchen, she was the boss.

I kept my arms around Vaughn's neck as he carried me into the living room. Until we'd entered, I worried about how to explain Mr. McMichael's presence to Charlie, but at least that one problem seemed to have solved itself. The room was empty.

Vaughn set me in Duke's wheelchair. "Where do you want to be?"

"Next to the window," I said. I waited while he moved the Queen Anne chair out of the way to make space. He rolled the wheelchair into the spot, and I held back the sheer curtains and peered outside.

It took me a moment to identify which window belonged to the Estabrooks. Earlier, the buildings across the street were dark, save for that one apartment, but now, a few neighbors were present. Tina, the owner of Tina's Salon, stood in front of a mirror and rolled her streaky blond hair into Velcro curlers. Tina had the best hair in all of San Ladrón, which kept her salon at the top of the list when it came to ranking the many that existed. I never could justify the number of beauty parlors in town, but somehow they each found enough of a customer base to stay in business.

A few doors down, Earl, the owner of Earl of Sandwich, was assessing his profile in a full-length mirror. He'd recently expanded his menu to include a variety of plant-based meats and actively targeted the health-conscious community by marketing himself in a series of before-and-after photos. Earl had dropped thirty pounds, and he attributed it all to his new offerings. The last time I stopped in for a sandwich, he told me sales were up thirty percent.

Next to Earl of Sandwich was Little Tony's Ristorante. Formerly known as Antonio's, the name changed when Tony Junior took over the family business. It was a white-napkin restaurant that catered to a date-night crowd. Inside, a man in a white T-shirt and painter's pants stood on a drop cloth rolling paint onto the walls.

"Odd day to paint," I said.

"Not if you own a restaurant. Today's the one day nobody expects a restaurant to be open."

"Tina's doing her hair," I pointed out.

"Hairstyling isn't just a job for Tina. It's a way of life." Vaughn lowered himself to the sofa next to me and stared outside. "You really think something funny happened over there?"

"'Funny' might not be the word I'd use."

"Tell me again what transpired."

I stared across the street into the windows above the Broadside Tavern. Sure enough, Mrs. Estabrook was moving around the kitchen. A large Dutch oven sat on the table behind her. Genevieve had one like it in the kitchen that she had brought to boil her potatoes, and it had taken both of us to carry it up my stairs. It easily weighed close to twenty pounds.

If that had fallen on Mrs. Estabrook's foot, she sure recovered quickly.

I was so lost in my thoughts that I didn't register the

sound of a toilet flushing or the fact that everybody I expected at my place was present and accounted for until I heard the one sentence I'd been hoping wouldn't be spoken.

"What are *you* doing here?" Charlie asked.

6

MR. MCMICHAEL AND CHARLIE FACED EACH OTHER. FOR a successful businessman who had experience in some of the biggest boardrooms in the greater Los Angeles area, he looked a little intimidated. He recovered quickly. "Charlie," he said. "Vaughn said you might be here."

The first thing I learned after moving to a small town was that people had secrets. The second thing I learned was that those secrets made life messy and complicated. And in Charlie's case, I learned not to get involved.

"This apartment's too crowded for me," she said. She held up the flat tire from Duke's spare wheelchair. "If anybody needs me, I'll be at my shop patching this." She left.

The thing nobody wants to admit about Thanksgiving is that it often brings together a group of people who would otherwise not choose to spend their time in close quarters. Families don't come with neat instructions for assembly, and messy differences, long since suppressed, can bubble up to the surface. Even with rules in place to avoid conversation about religion and politics, there are conversational landmines aplenty. You never knew when one might detonate. I could be mad at Charlie for leaving, but I could also see that by walking away, she allowed the rest of us to go on with our day.

"Vaughn, we should go," Mr. McMichael said.

"No," I said impulsively. "Stay. Genevieve's making plenty of food, and I'm not going to be any help."

"Are you implying my dad and I should stay here and work?" Vaughn asked. There was a sparkle in his eyes.

My eyes widened with the realization that it was exactly what I'd implied. "I didn't mean—"

"It's a good idea." Mr. McMichael picked up an apron from an assortment I'd made out of Thanksgiving-themed quilting cottons and tied it around his waist. "How can I assist?"

It took me a moment to recover from the image of Vic McMichael with a rooster-themed apron knotted over his dress slacks. "Genevieve's the boss," I finally said. "Check in with her."

Vaughn's dad left the living room. I stared at the doorframe, still not quite believing the richest man in San

Ladrón was in my kitchen wearing an apron I'd made out of fabric scraps just yesterday.

"Did that just happen?" I asked Vaughn.

"He's not a monster."

"I didn't mean to imply that he was. I only wish Charlie didn't leave."

"Charlie will come around. Some things can't be rushed."

I sat back in the wheelchair and stared idly out the window. Tina was still styling her hair. She picked up what looked like a footlong clipping of fringe and held it across the back of her head from ear to ear.

"Do me a favor?" I asked Vaughn. "Can you bring me the binoculars from the hall closet? They're in a burgundy case."

"If you weren't indisposed with that ankle, I'd probably give you a lecture about privacy laws."

"Then I'm thankful for my ankle."

Vaughn retrieved the binoculars, and I used them to zoom in on Tina. In the brief amount of time that had passed, her hair appeared to have grown by six inches. I lowered the binoculars. "Tina's hair isn't real."

"Let me see." Vaughn took the binoculars and looked across the street. After a few seconds, he lowered the binoculars. "Who knew? Tina wears extensions."

I took the binoculars and stared back into her apartment. Using nothing but her fingers and a couple of mirrors, she attached a long fringe of hair to the back of her head. She separated the locks and rolled each one in a Velcro roller like the one on top of her head. I lowered the binoculars.

"Her hair is famous. People travel from Los Angeles to come to her salon. What would happen if they knew it wasn't real?"

"Could be she's testing out a product. The extensions make her hair longer, but she's got a healthy mane as is." He raised the binoculars and looked again, then dropped them almost immediately. "Oh. Wow."

I took them and looked back at Tina. Even though her curtains were open, she'd taken off her robe and stood in her bra and panties. Tina had a couple of other assets that may have contributed to her popularity, and right now, they were pushed up and on display. I glanced at Vaughn, who had turned pink with embarrassment.

"She could close her curtains," he said.

"And not enjoy the glorious weather?" I asked. "Not a chance."

I raised the lenses and scanned the other street-facing windows. Like Tina, Earl was also in a state of undress. "Oh. Wow," I said.

"What?"

I handed Vaughn the binoculars. "Earl."

Vaughn peered at Earl's windows and immediately

lowered the binoculars. "A warning would have been nice."

"Look again. Earl's wearing a—a *girdle.*"

Vaughn raised the binoculars to his eyes a second time. He handed them back to me, and this time I watched as Earl peeled down a tight undergarment. His belly relaxed over his waistband—a far cry from a thirty-pound weight loss.

"He's faking his new body. His whole marketing campaign is a lie!"

Spying on the neighbors was great fun, and Vaughn and I took turns with the binoculars. In addition to Tina and Earl, we spotted a local author who usually sat in a booth in the back of the coffee shop and wrote each morning, staring dejectedly at the Closed sign on the door, and a couple of neighbors walking their dogs. Otherwise, the street was empty.

While Vaughn and I took turns with the binoculars, Pins, my furry gray tabby cat, jumped up on my lap. He nosed my elbow and relaxed after I stroked his fur. The layers of ivory chiffon and netting of my dress surrounded him, and he swatted at it. I picked him up and handed him to Vaughn, covered my lap in a throw blanket, and took Pins back. The blanket wasn't as appealing as the dress, though, so he left my lap and settled onto Vaughn's.

Unable to do much more than sit by the window and

stare outside, I found it funny to discover the secrets of my neighbors. I couldn't wait to tease Earl the next time I stopped in for a turkey sandwich. I looked lower to check on the status of Little Tony's Ristorante. The painter had moved onto a different wall. He paused and assessed his work then set the roller on a table and disappeared out of sight.

While I kept my vigil, a small white van drove down the street. I normally might not have noticed it, but today, there was no other traffic. The logo on the side said Special Delivery. There were words underneath, too small to read from my perch, but I knew what they were—"Have we got a package for you!"—because I'd seen this van before.

Special Delivery was a small regional delivery service. The owner had been involved in the business involving Genevieve's husband, and I hadn't expected to see him again since then. I turned up the magnification of the binoculars and watched the driver's-side door.

A gray-haired man in a uniform got out. I didn't recognize him. He tucked a medium-sized cardboard box under his arm and glanced at Tina's building, then turned to the right and walked two doors down. He stopped outside the Broadside Tavern and double-checked the number on the door against the package he carried.

Another car drove down the street, temporarily

blocking my view. When it passed, the deliveryman was gone.

7

"WHERE DID HE GO?" I ASKED.

"Who?" Vaughn said.

"The deliveryman." I pointed out the window. "He was carrying a box. He was outside Duke's place."

Vaughn took the binoculars and peered through them. I took the moment to appreciate his strong profile. "Uh-oh," he said.

"What?" I turned to the window, wondering what new secret Vaughn had seen. It wasn't anything inside another apartment that brought on Vaughn's response. It was the car parked on my side of the street and the two people who got out.

My parents.

"What are they doing here?" I asked.

Vaughn lowered the binoculars. “You didn’t invite them?”

“Of course, I *invited* them, but they turned me down. They’re leaving tomorrow for a pilgrimage to Philadelphia. My dad’s a real history buff.”

“You never told me that.”

“There’s a reason for that. Once you get him started, it’s almost impossible to get him to stop.”

Before I had a chance to explain why, I spotted Charlie coming out of her auto shop. She waved at my parents, and they waved back, and at least the answers to one of my questions became clear. Charlie had orchestrated this. She was making a point.

My parents lived roughly about thirty miles west in Burbank. On a day like today, with little to no traffic, they could make the drive in about half an hour. That’s approximately how much time had passed since Charlie discovered Vaughn and his dad in my apartment. Man, she worked fast.

I watched out the window as my parents waited for Charlie to catch up to them. Charlie had the wheel to Duke’s chair in her hand.

Uh-oh.

“Help me out of this chair,” I said to Vaughn.

“Why?”

“I don’t want my parents to know about my ankle.”

"Your foot is in a bucket of ice. I think they're going to figure it out."

The door downstairs opened, and the noisy sounds of footsteps on wooden stairs grew louder as they ascended. Vaughn was right; there was no point pretending I wasn't indisposed.

The landing atop the stairs led one of two directions. To the right was the bathroom and my bedroom. To the left was the kitchen and dining room, and through that was the living room where Vaughn and I sat. My mom and dad would know not to look for me in the bedroom, but they'd certainly consider turning around and going the other direction where they spotted Vic McMichael in my kitchen.

In an apron.

"Hello, Genevieve," my mom said. "It smells wonderful in here. And it's Duke, isn't it?"

"Yep," Duke said. "You remember Vic?"

"Of course. Hello, Vic."

"John, Helen."

"Where's Poly?" my dad asked.

"She's in the living room," Charlie said. "Let's go see her."

Seconds later, Charlie burst into the room with my parents behind her. She stepped to the side to reveal me. While the awkward small talk took place in the kitchen,

I'd covered my lap with the colorful crocheted blanket that I usually left draped along the back of the sofa. Needles, my orange tabby, had been asleep on it. He wasn't thrilled at having been woken and displaced, and he hopped onto the floor and licked at the condensation on the outside of the ice bucket.

"Look who I ran into," Charlie said.

I loved my parents. I loved seeing them, and I loved spending time with them. I had a happy childhood, and when I grew up, they tolerated my choice to take my degree from OTIS and work for a questionable pageant-dress company in Los Angeles's fabric district. They accepted my relationship with a finance guy who had dreams of becoming the next Richard Branson, and they supported my decision to leave him behind and move to San Ladrón after inheriting the shuttered business.

On any other day, I would have thrown my arms around them and expressed my gratitude for the unexpected visit, but there were several factors that kept me from doing so at the moment.

"She doesn't look happy to see us," my dad said to my mom.

"Don't get up," my mom said to me, making her point known through her tone of voice.

I pulled off the metaphorical Band-Aid and flung the blanket from my lap, revealing creamy chiffon, squished onto the seat of Duke's wheelchair, and the white bucket of ice where my foot was submerged. I raised my leg, slowly pulling my foot out of the slushy ice. My mom's eyes widened at the sight of my thick ankle.

"What happened?"

"I fell down the stairs," I said. I shot a quick glance at Charlie, challenging her not to reveal which stairs I'd fallen down.

She crossed the room and assessed my foot. "It looks awfully swollen. Shouldn't you go the emergency room?"

"It's not broken," I said. "It hurt like the dickens when it happened. You know if it's broken, it goes numb."

"She's right, Helen," my dad said. "Remember when she twisted her ankle in third grade?"

"I was thinking about her junior high accident," my mom replied.

"Then there was that time in college," my dad added.

They both turned their attention back to me. "Poly, you really do need to slow down," my mom said. "The world will wait for you."

"It's easy for you two to slow down. You're both retired. I have things to do, people to see."

"Like the Estabrooks," Charlie said under her breath.

I shot her another glare.

"Hi, Helen, John," Vaughn said. He stood and shook my dad's hand. My mom pulled him in for a hug. "I'm glad you're joining us. Poly said you're leaving for Pennsylvania in the morning. I'd love to hear what you have planned."

Vaughn vacated the seat next to me to join my dad on the other side of the room. My mom came over to me, and Charlie followed.

"Is that Millie's *Rear Window* dress?"

"Yes," I said. "I found it in the back of the closet. The skirt had some damage to it, but I found a similar chiffon in the inventory and replaced two layers."

"I hate to ask this, but can you stand?"

It was as good a time as any to test my ankle. I braced myself on the arms of the wheelchair and pushed myself up to a standing position. The creamy folds of fabric fell into place.

It didn't surprise me that my great-aunt Millie had made a replica of Grace Kelly's famous dress. My aunt had taught me how to sew at an early age, and part of that education had been how to deconstruct vintage garments and use them to make patterns. Thanks to her, I fell in love with styles from the thirties and forties, garments she'd been able to procure cheaply from secondhand shops in the fifties and sixties. It was that love of thirties glamour that led me to design pageant dresses, though my old cheapskate boss dumbed them down with flammable fabric and gaudy embellishments.

But this dress was a marvel. The bodice was black,

fitted to my rib cage, with a wide V-neck in both the front and the back. It had short sleeves that fit snuggly against my arms and a snatched waist set off with a thin black patent belt and jet-beaded vines appliqued down onto the full ivory skirt.

I didn't know how many layers of chiffon the original dress had, but mine had twelve. Twelve layers of sheer chiffon, enough to make it opaque. The skirt landed at an unusual tea length, a few inches above my ankle. Had I chosen to wear a gown, I may have been able to hide the bucket underneath.

"It's magnificent," she said. "But it's torn."

"Where?"

She pointed to my hip. I glanced down and saw the damage, a long, diagonal gash in one of the panels I'd recently replaced.

"I'll fix it later."

As I lowered myself back into the chair, Vaughn's dad entered the room with a tray of glasses. He offered the tray to my dad first. Mr. McMichael was older than my dad, and while the history between our families was water under the bridge, all it would take was a downpour to flood the banks. I held my breath and waited until my dad took a glass. Vaughn seemed to exhale too. Mr. McMichael circled around to me, my mom, and finally, Charlie, who remained stalwart in favor of Thanksgiving discourse.

Genevieve poked her head into the room. “We’re eating in an hour.”

The arrival of my parents had distracted me from my window vigil. My mother, the eagle eye, pulled the binoculars out from between the sofa cushions. “Poly, is there something you want to tell us?”

8

FIFTEEN MINUTES LATER, MY MOTHER HANDED THE binoculars off to my dad while I tried to convince them that something fishy was going on across the street.

"It looks like a woman making Thanksgiving dinner," she said. She turned toward the kitchen. "Genevieve? Can you spare a minute?"

Genevieve entered the room. Her soft blond hair hung in curls around her peaches-and-cream complexion. Her cheeks were flushed from the heat in the kitchen, which enhanced her cherubic appearance. She'd lost a few pounds after her marriage dissolved, but a trip to Paris to learn to make authentic French pastries had helped to put them back on her frame.

Today she wore a navy-blue cashmere sweater and

pleated trousers. Her apron was yellow toile with depictions of French countryside in blue.

"Yes?"

"How's it going?" I asked.

"Fine. I've got two efficient helpers. I told Vic if investment banking doesn't work out for him, he can prep food in my kitchen."

Charlie snorted.

My mother handed Genevieve the binoculars. "Do you see anything unusual in the apartment across the street?"

"The Estabrooks?" she asked. She raised the binoculars to her eyes.

"You met them?"

"They came into my shop last week. You know me, I like to chat with people, and when I meet someone new, I always try to find out where they're headed or where they're from. She said something about them moving here, but he cut her off before we could keep talking." She lowered the binoculars. "I remember thinking it was rude of him, but I'm sensitive to overbearing men." She handed the binoculars to me. "The only unusual thing I see is that she appears to be making Thanksgiving dinner for one."

"Her husband's asleep in the bedroom," I said. "At least that's what she told Sheriff Clark."

As soon as I said it, I regretted it. My call to Clark

could have remained known to Charlie and Vaughn, and it would have been best to keep it that way. But cats let out of bags don't like to go back in them.

"Charlie's Sheriff Clark?" Genevieve asked. She went back into the kitchen.

"He's not my Sheriff Clark," Charlie said to anyone who would listen.

"He could be," I said, a mediocre attempt at diversion.

"You and Sheriff Clark?" my dad said. "That's nice."

Vaughn and his dad had the good sense not to say anything.

My mother reached up and brushed my bangs out of my eyes. With any luck, she was distracted by my need for a trim. She cocked her head to the side and assessed me. "What's this about Sheriff Clark?"

"It sounds suspicious, right?" I said after bringing my guests up to speed. "Mrs. Estabrook didn't answer the door when we knocked, and she didn't check on the noise in the hallway. She told Sheriff Clark the thud I heard was a Dutch oven falling on her foot, but she isn't limping." I pointed out the window. "Her Dutch oven is one of those cast-iron ones. They weigh about twenty pounds."

Genevieve picked up the binoculars and looked back

out the window. "I dropped one of those on my big toe once and broke it."

"See?" I said to the rest of the group. "That woman's story is suspicious."

"You know what's more suspicious?" my dad said. "She appears to be making a ham."

The rest of the group chimed in, poking fun at the story I'd invented around the Estabrooks. Even Duke got into things, calling out from the kitchen, "It was Mrs. Estabrook in the kitchen with the lead pipe!"

It was one thing to host Thanksgiving dinner and have someone else cook it for you. It was quite another to not be able to get up and leave.

While the rest of the group brainstormed wild theories about what might have happened across the street, my cell phone buzzed. I pulled it out and immediately recognized the number of my Monday appointment. Happy for the excuse to tune everybody out, I answered.

"Poly, this is Scott Forester. We spoke about your fabric. My morning appointment canceled on me. I'm in your neighborhood. I know it's a holiday, but is there any chance you can see me today?"

"How long until you're here?"

"Ten minutes."

I did some quick calculations. Ten minutes to his arrival, twenty minutes to assess my inventory and make me an offer, back upstairs by the time Duke was slicing

Genevieve's turkey. Barring any unforeseen problems, I could make it work.

"Let's do it," I said. We reconfirmed my address, and I hung up. It wasn't until that moment that I remembered my ankle, the wheelchair, and the need to ask for help to get downstairs to my shop.

The problems, which were stacking up like hits at Motown, grew.

Vaughn and my dad were deep in conversation across the room, probably something about Betsy Ross, or maybe Ben Franklin. Vaughn had a glazed-over look on his face, though I doubted my dad recognized it. I turned to my mom. "Do you see what I see?" I asked. I pointed across the room.

"It's nice that they get along so well," she said.

That didn't work.

"Charlie?" I bellowed. I didn't know where she was, but as far as I was concerned, she owed me. My phone buzzed again. It was her. "Where are you?"

"Downstairs with your cats. It's too crowded up there."

"Do you have any interest in pretending you work for me?"

"What's the pay?"

"I'll let you stay for dinner."

"That's Frenchy's call, not yours."

"It's my apartment."

"It's her food."

I sacrificed the argument for a chance to win the war. "My Monday appointment is going to be here any minute. He's interested in the bolts of sheer fabric stacked by the bottom of the stairs. Can you handle it?"

"Sure," she said.

I expected a little resistance, and Charlie's amenable response sent up a warning flare.

"You know what? I'll ask Vaughn to help me down the stairs. If I take too long, you can start eating without me."

"Gotta go," Charlie said. "There's someone at the gate."

My mother patted my knee. "See? You don't have to do everything yourself. Maybe this ankle situation was a blessing in disguise. Now tell me, when's the last time you had a trim?"

9

"THIRTY MINUTES!" GENEVIEVE CALLED OUT FROM THE kitchen, which was quickly followed with, "Not that one, Vic! The *other* blue-and-white bowl. Helen? Can you and John set the table? Not yet, Duke!"

Freed from the lesson of the history of Thanksgiving, Vaughn joined me by the window. "Any status reports?"

"Charlie's downstairs with my fabric buyer, and my mom thinks I need a haircut."

"I meant with the Estabrooks."

I didn't say anything right away. There were a lot of people in my apartment, more than I could remember being there all at once since I moved in. The promise of eating the meal we'd smelled all morning was becoming a reality. Most of my guests had gathered in the kitchen as if their presence would speed things up. The living room was quiet. Nice. But even nicer was how Vaughn treated my theories as possible.

Vaughn's hair was freshly cut into a short style that required minimal fuss. He hadn't shaved today, and he had a light scruff on his cheeks and chin. His green eyes were rimmed with gold and shot through with flecks of the same. They reflected the bright sunlight coming from the windows.

"You believe me, don't you?" I asked.

"I think things across the street are a little suspicious."

I picked up the binoculars and handed them to him. "Tell me what you see."

He raised them to his eyes. "Mrs. Estabrook is in her kitchen. She just checked her oven. Her table is set for two. The taper candles on the table have burned down about two inches." He lowered the binoculars and looked at me. "Maybe that could be us someday."

I reached my hand out and placed it on top of Vaughn's. His skin was warm from the sun filtering through the window. He turned his hand over and curled his fingers around mine.

"I'd like that," I said. My heart ticked faster, and the inconvenience of an apartment filled with uninvited guests who barely suppressed their thoughts about each other fell away. For the briefest moment, it was just Vaughn and me, alone, our knees touching while we held hands and enjoyed an unexpectedly sunny Thursday afternoon.

A cloud moved across the sun, temporarily darkening the room. With it came a shadow across Vaughn's face. A flash of lightning filled the sky, followed by a clap of thunder. I turned away from Vaughn to the window in time to see the predicted rainstorm commence.

A sheet of angry, diagonal dashes fell from the sky. Gone was the bright, sunny morning and clear blue sky. Clouds continued to move in, darkening the street. In the span of five minutes, the scene out the window went from day to night.

Movement on the sidewalk caught my attention. A man ran from my shop doors to a small van parked alongside the curb. He held something brown, flat, and rectangular over his head. It was the cardboard at the center of a bolt of fabric that indicated the brand and design name, the content mix, and the price. The man must have been my appointment. A few seconds later, his van started. He pulled away from the curb and drove down the street. I hoped Charlie had the foresight to have him pull around the back of the shop to load the sheer fabric inventory—or better yet, to have him return after we'd bagged it in plastic to keep it from getting damaged by the rain. I started to stand, forgetting about my ankle for a moment, ready to go take care of things when pain shot through the network of nerves in my leg. Nausea socked me in the gut a second later, and I dropped back onto the chair.

Downstairs, the retractable gate rattled into place. Footsteps clomped up the stairs. The oven opened and closed, and Genevieve's voice said, "If you've been working on cars, you better wash up now, Charlie. We're eating in fifteen minutes."

"Where's Polyester?" Charlie asked.

"With Vaughn in the living room."

Vaughn and I were still holding hands when Charlie came in. "That was fast," I said. "Is he coming back when the rain lets up?"

"He's not interested," she said. "He said it wasn't what he wanted, and he's annoyed that you wasted his time."

"It's *exactly* what he wanted. You let him leave?" I asked. Without thinking about it, I pulled my hand away from Vaughn. "It was all worked out. I sent him pictures and described it in detail. I gave him a fair price. It was practically a done deal. He was going to drop off a check and take it with him."

"Whoa," Charlie said. She held up both hands and stepped backward. "Dude changed his mind. People do that."

"But I need the money. And I need the space. And I can't do anything with this stupid ankle in this stupid bucket of ice." I kicked my foot out in front of me. The bucket tipped. The ice had melted since first being placed in the bucket, and slushy water spilled out across my Persian rug. If left unattended, not only would it damage the rug, but it would destroy the hardwood underneath. I raised my foot and hopped to the pile of aprons. I launched them across the room onto the wet spill. I hopped back and dropped down to all fours, trying to sop up the water as it ran in different directions. My frustration mounted. Losing out on the potential sale, twisting my ankle, being relegated to Duke's wheelchair, and spending all my time inventing a narrative about the couple in the apartment across the street...if it hadn't been Thanksgiving, I would have taken a bath in my claw-footed tub and crawled into bed with a book. I would have written today off and started fresh tomorrow. This was one more thing that made me feel trapped.

"Poly," Vaughn said. He got down on the floor and put his hand on top of mine. "I'll handle the spill."

"Time to eat!" Genevieve called out from the kitchen. I pulled myself up from the floor and onto the sofa. The binoculars dug into my thigh. I pulled them out from under me and was about to pack them back into their case when I saw something I never could have predicted outside of Duke's bar.

Despite the ominous weather conditions and the lit tapers burning down on her tabletop, Mrs. Estabrook had left her apartment and was hurrying down the street.

10

THE NEWLY DARKENED SKIES AND PREPONDERANCE OF rain made it difficult to make out details, but there was no denying that the same woman who had been inside the apartment over Duke's tavern had just left the premises and was hurrying down Bonita Avenue. She wore a khaki trench coat over her black turtleneck and pants, and it swung loosely around her torso. Her hands were in tight balls, pumping on either side of her body. She leaned into the rain, taking long strides as if there was somewhere she had to get to quickly despite the unfavorable weather conditions.

I turned to Vaughn to tell him what I saw. He was on his hands and knees, spreading out colorful aprons across the floor, corralling partially melted ice into a pile and transferring it back into the bucket. I looked at the dining room. Genevieve stood in the doorway, watching me.

"We're waiting for you," she said. Her voice sounded tense. Wisps of blond hair had escaped her low bun, and tendrils curled around her face. The flush from the hot oven left her in a perpetual state of rosy. Her toile apron was coated on one side with flour. Compared to how I would have looked after cooking dinner for ~~four~~ ~~six~~ eight, she was ready to enter a beauty pageant.

"Mrs. Estabrook left her apartment," I said. I pointed at the window over my shoulder. "And her oven's still on."

My dad poked his head around the corner of the doorframe. "Enough is enough, Poly. The meal is ready. We're all waiting for you and Vaughn."

I glanced at Vaughn. While I'd been staring out the window, he'd been taking care of the spilled bucket. Nobody had been looking outside except for me.

Was this all in my imagination? Mrs. Estabrook leaving her apartment in the rain looked suspicious, but if her husband *was* sick at the apartment, then couldn't she have been on her way to pick up some medicine? Was it safe to leave him alone with the oven on and the candles burning? A person would have to be desperate to leave their apartment now, in this sudden storm.

I didn't even know this woman, and nobody believed me anyway. And it wasn't like I could do anything about what I thought I saw. Sheriff Clark had checked it out and said there was nothing more he could do. My ankle was the size of Genevieve's turkey. I needed to shake off my suspicions and enjoy Thanksgiving dinner with my friends and family.

I stood on my good leg and winced from the pain. I dropped back onto the worn sofa cushions and held my injured leg in front of me. My dad whistled at the sight of my swollen ankle. "You need to see a doctor."

"It's just a sprain," I said. "You said it yourself: sprained ankles hurt. Broken ankles go numb. As long as it hurts, there's nothing I can do but ice it and elevate it and wait until the swelling goes down."

"I don't know, Poly. It looks awfully big."

I flapped my hand to wave away his concerns. "I've caused enough interruptions already. This isn't the first time I've twisted my ankle, and it probably won't be the last."

Genevieve joined my dad in the doorway. "Are you coming?"

I got back into Duke's wheelchair, and Vaughn rolled me to the dining room entrance. Duke had started carving the rosemary-and-sage-rubbed turkey while Genevieve filled serving bowls with fresh cranberry sauce, gravy, corn, Brussels sprouts, and mashed potatoes. A basket was filled with steaming biscuits. Bottles of Sancerre sat along the apricot-hued table runner, interspersed with bottles of Badoit. Mr. McMichael picked up a bottle of wine and filled each of the glasses. He appeared to be unaware of my wild theories about the apartment across the street, and, for the moment, I did nothing to clue him in.

I'd originally expected four people for the day, but Vaughn and his dad made six. My parents brought the number to eight. Genevieve had planned to make far more food than we could eat in five meals, so stretching the meal was not an issue, but seating was.

"Dad, take my place. There's not enough room at the table for everybody. I need to wrap my ankle, so I'll do that now and eat when everybody's done."

"I'll help you," Vaughn said. I glanced at him, ready to reject his offer, but he had a strained look on his face, and I couldn't read his expression.

"Okay," I said, simply because it was the fastest way to move the agenda along.

I put my arms around Vaughn's neck, and he lifted me out of Duke's wheelchair. My dad and mom shared a predictable look. Again, I felt Vaughn's hands through the fabric of my dress, and I felt a little bad that the burden of carrying me across the street and now into my bedroom fell to him.

There was one way to the bandages, and it was through the dining room. To clear the path, everyone took their seats. My mom was between my dad and Vaughn's dad, probably her way of mitigating a potential clash of personalities. Duke was at the head of the table, and Genevieve was to his left. Charlie was next to Gen, which left her directly across from Mr. McMichael. As soon as she realized it, she stood back up, but the table was full, and there were no other seats to claim.

Charlie glared at me. I wasn't in a position to say or do anything about the seating arrangements, and I saw no point making Mr. McMichael feel any less welcome than he'd already been made to feel. "There's a roll of quilt batting in my bedroom," I said to Vaughn. "We can wrap it in that."

Once Vaughn and I were into the bedroom, the sounds of serving spoons against dishes replaced the conversation in the dining room. Vaughn set me on the edge of my bedspread, a faded pink-and-white coverlet Aunt Millie had made from scraps of fabric.

People with talent can make something out of nothing, and while Aunt Millie had a knack for running the fabric store, her truest talent lay in creating. This whole apartment was filled with touches like this: pillows, rag rugs, blankets.

And the contents of her closet.

When I first moved back into the apartment, I'd marveled at the clothes that still hung behind the sliding closet doors. Millie had taught me to love and respect garments from previous decades, and because of that, I was able to quickly recognize the eras from which her original (tattered) and replicated garments belonged. The largest portion of her closet was dedicated to the thirties: embellished suits and gowns, soft, feminine shoulders and slim silhouettes that predated the structure and volume that came in the forties. There were feathers as trim, and paillettes stitched onto collar points and cuffs. There was trapunto stitching, neat rows of parallel lines that set off waists and cuffs. Blouses made from organdy or silk, trimmed with ruffled collars and thin string bows at the neck hung in a collection that ranged from yellow to purple, some with floral or geometric patterns. The condition of the clothes indicated two things: Aunt Millie had known how to construct a garment, and Aunt Millie had enjoyed her wardrobe.

Over time, I came to identify pieces from the patchwork coverlet on my bed in garments in the closet. The pink silk also lined a black-and-white tweed jacket. The pink floral had been used in a loose summer dress. The sheer pink dotted Swiss was a long-sleeved blouse that tied with a matching bow at the neck, helping the collar to stand up, where it peeked out of the jewel-neck collar of a soft mauve swing coat and matching pencil skirt.

When I reopened the fabric store, I'd found a back room filled with old, dusty inventory. There was a very good reason for the room to have been sealed, and as a member of the family, I might have agreed with my great-uncle Marius's decision, but as the new owner of the store, I had to think differently. Fabric is meant to be appreciated, to be felt, observed, touched, enjoyed. It did nothing to have a stockroom full of vintage fabrics, not if they were left to rot in poor conditions. For the first six months that Material Girl was open, I relied heavily on the unique value proposition of carrying material from a time gone by. It got me attention, but after the initial rush of costumers from Los Angeles bought out what they could use to source upcoming movies, I was left with slim pickings. The corner of sheer fabrics was the largest glut of unsellable fabrics in my inventory, and it had been with more than a little reluctance that I faced the inevitable fact that my best course of action was to sell them off to a jobber.

The tactile feel of the old coverlet under my hand transported me to a whole different set of problems, and I forgot all about my painful ankle until Vaughn brought me back to the present. I'd instructed him to the closet, where a puffy roll of batting sat inside the doors, and then to the third drawer of my bathroom vanity where I kept a spare pair of scissors too dull to use on fabric. I placed my foot on a stool I kept by the side of my bed so Pins and Needles had an easier time jumping on the comforter, and Vaughn pulled the stool closer and sat facing me. He gingerly positioned my heel on his thigh and touched the taut skin around my ankle. I winced.

"Still hurts?" he asked.

"Still hurts."

"Sounds like it's not your first sprain."

"You don't grow up uncoordinated and never twist your ankle. This is the third or fourth time. I've lost count." I gave him a wry smile.

"Then we need to make sure it's secure. The more times you reinjure it, the less likely it'll fully recover."

I didn't like the sound of that, but I wasn't in a position to argue with him. I leaned back on my hands and pressed my lips together while he wound the cotton batting around my foot, ankle, and midcalf. By the time he was done, my ankle was immobile.

"Tell me again what happened at Duke's earlier today."

"When I fell?"

"How you fell, what happened after. The whole story."

"According to everybody else, there's nothing to tell."

"I'm not interested in their opinions. I'm interested in yours."

Vaughn had a way of making me feel like the most important person in the room, but I didn't think this was simply a gesture of romance. I thought back to that moment after I fell down the stairs, after Charlie left with

Duke's flat tire, when I was stranded all alone in Duke's office.

"Duke told us he got the apartment over his bar up to code and rented it out to a regional sales rep and her husband. Charlie and I took a muffin basket to them as a welcome to the neighborhood gesture."

"You sure it wasn't a nosy neighbor gesture?"

I smiled wryly. "It was a little of both, I guess. When we got there, I heard voices arguing through the door, but when I knocked, nobody answered. We left the basket out front, and I fell down the stairs."

Vaughn's face flinched as if he empathically felt the impact of my tumble. He secured the batting with small metal butterfly clips and rested his hands on either side of my leg. "What next?"

"Charlie helped me into Duke's spare wheelchair. One of the tires was flat, so she left to get a bicycle pump. I called Duke to let him know what happened, and while we were on the phone, I heard a loud thud overhead."

"Describe the thud."

"According to everybody else, it was a run-of-the-mill thud."

"And according to you?"

I felt heat climb my cheeks. "It sounded like a body."

He nodded as if that wasn't the craziest thing I could have said. He tapped my ankle with his index fingers. "Feel that?"

"Barely."

"Good. If you promise to slow down for the rest of the day, I'll escort you out front for your Thanksgiving meal."

"I suppose I don't have much of a choice."

Vaughn stood and held out his hand. I used it to leverage myself up to a standing position and bent my knee to keep my wrapped ankle from touching the ground. Needles ran into the room and sniffed my leg. A piece of batting stuck out from the bottom, and he swatted it. His claws got caught in the white fluff, and he jerked his limb to disengage it. I bent down and freed his claws then scooped him up and held him against the bodice of my dress. I felt something tug on the hem of my dress on the other side and looked down in time to see Pins starting to chew on the lining. I set Needles on the bed and scooped up Pins. "No," I said and kissed him between his ears, effectively negating my reprimand. I set him on the bed next to Needles, who swatted Pins on the head.

I left the cats in the bedroom and put my arm around Vaughn's shoulders while he kept his arm around my waist. Vaughn was six feet to my five feet nine, and after a lifetime of towering over my dates, looking up at him was refreshing. He assisted me down the hall and through the dining room. Conversation had abated while the group shared in the delights of Genevieve's meal.

"I fixed you each a plate," Genevieve said. "They're in the oven."

"We'll eat in the living room," I said.

Vaughn guided me back to Duke's wheelchair next to the window. Genevieve followed with two plates piled high with food. I pointed to two collapsible TV trays that were tucked next to my bookcase, and after Vaughn helped me sit, he retrieved the trays and set them up in front of us. Genevieve set our plates on each. Charlie followed with two glasses of wine, each filled to the brim. She took a sizeable gulp from one and handed it to me.

The severe storm had let up, replaced by a steady downpour. Puddles accumulated by the sidewalks, flowing toward the drains in urgent streams. The binoculars were wedged between the cushion and the arm of the sofa, and I pulled them out. Before I set them down, I raised them back to my eyes and looked across the street. I hoped to see Mr. and Mrs. Estabrook sitting down for their Thanksgiving meal.

But what I saw brought back every one of my suspicions instead.

11

"TWO MEN JUST CARRIED A ROLLED-UP CARPET OUT OF the Estabrook's apartment," I said to Vaughn.

Charlie snatched the binoculars from me and looked for herself. "You're right."

"I'm calling Clark," I said. This time she didn't protest.

It must have been a slow day at the sheriff's office because Sheriff Clark didn't waste time reminding me of the restrictions of his job. After hearing the latest development, Clark agreed to check things out and report to us when he was done.

Unfortunately, Clark wasn't the only one who had a reason to respond. When I hung up from the call, Duke was in his wheelchair in the doorway. "I don't believe this," he said. "You of all people should know how hard it is to be the new person in a small town." He wheeled himself in a circle. "Sorry, Genevieve. The food was wonderful, but I can't stay. Vic, can you help me down the stairs?"

I tried to stand, to race after him, but I wasn't going anywhere. Vaughn grabbed my hand, and I squeezed it—hard—and bit my lip to keep from crying out. I dropped back down and released his hand. He stood and followed Duke. "Dad, maybe we should go too. Duke, I'll help you down the stairs." He turned around and gave me a secret smile, but not before I saw him massaging his hand where I'd gripped it.

The apartment was quiet save for the sounds of Vaughn, his dad, and Duke descending the stairs. In the dining room, Genevieve was left with my mom and dad. Charlie was with me, but we'd said very little to each other since she botched my appointment with the potential fabric buyer.

"You're not kidding about this, are you?" Charlie said.

"You were with me at her door. We heard voices but nobody answered. Nobody came to check out the noise when I fell down the stairs. Both of those things are a little weird, but not unexplainable."

"But you heard something."

"I heard a thud. It wasn't the sound a Dutch oven makes when it falls to the ground. It was—" I searched for a description of the sound I'd heard—"less localized. More dull."

"Like a body," she said. I studied her expression, expecting to find her making fun of me. She held up her hands. "No judgment here. If anybody else told me they heard a body drop, I'd question their sanity. You've earned some credibility."

"Gee, thanks," I said.

"It wasn't a dig. There's a reason Clark takes you seriously."

I picked up the binoculars and looked out the window. Vaughn was across the street, holding the door open while Vic pushed Duke into his bar. Clark parked his sheriff's SUV alongside the curb next to them. The entire view was gray thanks to the rainfall.

People who say it never rains in Southern California are wrong. It is true that we spend a lot of time in a drought state and live under guidelines to water our lawns every other day and keep showers under fifteen minutes, but the truth of the matter is that when it does rain, it pours.

Summers are the worst, and by the time the weather breaks in November, we're desperate for the climate to change. The problem is we're ill-equipped for the rain when it finally comes.

Water pinged off Sheriff Clark's hat and uniform. By next month, he'd wear a plastic coat over his uniform or at least travel with a plastic poncho, but today he was caught unprepared. His sturdy boots sloshed through the cascade of water on the street, kicking up displaced puddles with each step. He caught the door as it was closing and entered behind Vic, Vaughn, and Duke.

Lights went on at the Broadside Tavern, but whatever the men did, their actions weren't conveniently located next to a street-facing window. I was sure something was wrong over there, but there was nothing I could do. Frustrated, I handed the binoculars to Charlie.

"Have at it," I said.

She took the binoculars and looked out the window. I turned around and bit into the roll on the side of my plate. My food had cooled, but it was delicious nonetheless. I sliced off a corner of turkey from the piece on my plate and savored the subtle nuances of butter, rosemary, and salt after placing it in my mouth. I temporarily forgot about the Estabrooks and followed the bite of turkey with a forkful of rich and creamy mashed potatoes, then sampled the fresh cranberry sauce. Genevieve had added orange zest, which expanded the flavor profile of the dish. After the cranberry sauce, I bit into a sage-rubbed biscuit. Genevieve had outdone herself with each dish. If the meal was this good, I couldn't wait to taste her pie.

"Huh," Charlie said next to me.

I swallowed a hefty bite of biscuit and turned back to her. "Huh what?"

"Big Joe and Maria just left Lopez Donuts."

"Why is that a 'huh'?"

"Big Joe told me they were going to spend Thanksgiving in Los Angeles. They were supposed to leave yesterday, but his van needs a new fan belt. I told him not to take any road trips until I had a chance to fix it."

"Big Joe got a last-minute order from the Waverly House for six dozen crullers. *He* understands that business owners sometimes work on holidays."

"Since when does the Waverly House order donuts?"

"Since their chef is busy making a six-course Thanksgiving dinner. Adelaide thought it would be easier to offer a donut buffet for breakfast and let Chef start his meal prep early."

In the year that I'd lived in San Ladrón, I'd come to know the habits of most of the businesses. Lopez Donuts was a fan favorite, as was the Waverly House, though they were at opposite ends of the culinary spectrum. That was one of the many things I'd come to love about San Ladrón, how there existed a mutual respect for what each person brought to the table—literally, in this case.

I took the binoculars from Charlie and stared at the car in front of the donut shop. Carlos and Antonio, the donut-shop owners' two boys, were clambering over each other in the back seat. Big Joe held an umbrella over his wife's head while she climbed into the passenger seat, then he walked around to the driver's side. The lights went on, but the car didn't start. Moments later, a plume of thick gray smoke poured from the hood.

12

CHARLIE CURSED. SHE HOPPED UP FROM THE SOFA AND ran out of the room. Her motorcycle boots pounded down my staircase—*clomp clomp clomp*—faster than I'd been going when I fell, thank you very much, but instead of losing her footing and crashing like me, she burst out of the shop entrance into the rain.

The storm had already subsided, trading the insistent rainfall for a steady patter of droplets dancing against the blacktop. Drops pinged off Charlie's head and shoulders as she raced down the street in the direction of Lopez Donuts. All four of the Lopezes now stood on the sidewalk. Maria and her two boys huddled together under the one umbrella, and Big Joe stood by the hood of the car, getting soaked. Charlie and Big Joe appeared to argue for a moment before he turned to his family and pointed to my side of the street. The umbrella kept me from seeing Maria's response, but she seemed to agree with whatever Big Joe said because the four of them ran across the street to my side. I had a sinking feeling I knew what Charlie had said to them, and I was proven right when the door downstairs opened and Big Joe's voice boomed up the stairs.

"Poly?"

"We're up here," Genevieve called. "Come join us!"

It was a good thing I had a plate of food in front of me because the leftovers I'd planned to eat all week were swiftly disappearing before my eyes.

If the sound of Charlie descending my wooden staircase was loud, then the sound of four Lopezes—two under the age of ten—ascending them was downright thunderous. There wasn't a whole lot I could do from my perch on the sofa, so I ate another bite of turkey and waited for someone to come in and keep me company.

"Have a seat," Genevieve said from the dining room. "Duke, Vic, and Charlie left, and nobody was in that seat at the end."

"Where's Poly?"

"In here," I called out.

"She twisted her ankle," my dad said.

"It might be broken," my mom added.

"It's not broken," I called out again. "It's not numb!"

"Whatever you say, Poly," my mom said.

It occurred to me that if I'd bothered to befriend a doctor in San Ladrón, he or she might have shown up for Thanksgiving, and the state of my ankle would be known once and for all.

Chairs were pulled out from the table, and just as it seemed as if I was destined to eat by myself, Maria Lopez carried her plate into the living room. In one head-to-toe scan, she assessed the situation. She scored points for not asking what happened.

"Where's Vaughn?" she asked after spotting the tray table set up next to mine.

"He and his dad helped Duke back to his bar."

"Why didn't they stay?"

I shrugged, at first attempting to downplay what had happened that morning. The two people who believed me were Charlie and Vaughn, neither of whom were here.

Genevieve entered the living room. "Didn't Poly tell you? She's playing Hitchcock today. She thinks she saw something nefarious happen across the street." She sat on the sofa across the room from me and set a glass of white wine on a coaster. She leaned forward and pulled a piece of blueberry buckle from the dish then bit off the tip.

Maria jumped to the wrong conclusion. "You already know Big Joe and I like to argue. It doesn't mean anything. I told him to get that car checked out. He said it was fine. Now I find out Charlie told him the fan belt was about to go. She warned him not to drive it until she replaced it. We're lucky it's raining out there! If that engine had caught fire on any other day, there's no telling what would have happened."

"Genevieve wasn't talking about you," I said. I rolled the wheelchair forward then attempted to maneuver it so I faced the window. I pointed directly across the street into the apartment above the Broadside Tavern.

"Duke rented his apartment to a couple from out of town. Charlie and I went over to invite them here, and nobody answered, and after I fell down the stairs, I heard a thud."

Maria set her fork down alongside her plate. "You want to fill in the details you skipped?" she asked. Her gaze tracked down to my foot and back up to my face. "If you want me to believe you, you're going to have to tell me everything."

FIFTEEN MINUTES LATER, Big Joe and my dad had moved my sofa from the window and set up a telescope given to me by my ex-boyfriend. It was among the few mementoes from that relationship that I'd kept, more because it was the one time he gave me something I wanted. We'd been living together in Los Angeles in an apartment with a flat roof where we could stare at the sky. Now that I lived in a Victorian apartment in San Ladrón, there was no good way to moon gaze.

The telescope was perfect for spying on the neighbors, though.

I stayed away from the window while Big Joe and my dad took peering across the street. Maria and my mom shared the binoculars. Genevieve was in the kitchen, making coffee and tea while Carlos and Antonio were in the bedroom with the cats.

I'd brought the newcomers up to speed: Charlie and my innocuous visit from the welcome wagon complete with a muffin basket, my fall down the stairs, the suspicious thud (I refused to call it anything else), and the routine visit from Clark. I added to it my new evidence: Mrs. Estabrook leaving her apartment in the middle of the thunderstorm and two men showing up to remove a rolled-up carpet from the premises. Individually, each item could be explained. Together, they convinced me more than ever that something was wrong.

"Are those the two men you saw carry the carpet?" Big Joe asked. I raised the binoculars. The two men came out of Little Tony's.

"Yes."

"Last time I was at the Broadside, Duke offered me

the carpet from his apartment. Mr. Estabrook didn't know if his wife would like it. I turned it down." At this, Maria's brow lowered over her eyes, and Big Joe added, "It's mauve. Wouldn't match our colors." Maria nodded, appeased. "I told Duke Little Tony was renovating his apartment, and he might want it. Could be Tony arranged to take it off their hands."

"Or it could be hiding Mr. Estabrook's body," I said.

"Poly!" Genevieve said sharply from the doorway. She held a freshly baked pumpkin pie with her oven-mitt-covered hands. "Must you be such a ghoul? You've had a house full of friends and family all day, and all you can do is stare out the window and imagine a woman killed her husband. Do you even hear yourself? Francis Estabrook is new to San Ladrón. She's alone with her husband. Maybe they *did* have a fight. Maybe she didn't want to move here. You look through those binoculars and you see a crime scene. Do you know what I see?"

I shook my head.

She slammed the pie on the counter and strode toward the window. She snatched the binoculars from my hands and looked outside. "I see a table set for two people. Two glasses of wine, two glasses of water, two place settings. I see a woman moving from the kitchen to the bedroom, probably telling her husband the meal is almost ready. Why can't you see that?"

I took the binoculars from her and looked out the

window again. I wanted to see everything Genevieve saw. And this time I did. I saw the table settings, the napkins, the goblets, the candles, and the wine.

I also saw a man in a purple sweater, the man we all knew as Mr. Estabrook, striding down the sidewalk toward the Broadside Tavern.

13

EVEN THOUGH THE RAIN GRAYED OUT THE COLORS ON THE street, Mr. Estabrook's purple sweater pierced the haze. The last time I'd seen that purple sweater was this morning, when I saw the argument between husband and wife. It was the argument that first piqued my curiosity about the two of them, before I suggested to Charlie that we head across the street and invite the Estabrooks to join our small party of four. Since then, our party had more than doubled, but not because the Estabrooks had said yes to my invitation.

"Poly, wasn't Mr. Estabrook wearing a purple sweater this morning?" Genevieve asked.

The last thing I wanted to admit aloud was that the suspected victim of my imagined homicide was on his way home, so I said nothing. The man slowed outside of the Broadside and looked up at the neon BAR sign. The rain grayed out my view, but I watched him pull open the door and disappear inside.

A few minutes later, Vaughn, his dad, and Sheriff Clark left the Broadside. Sheriff Clark said something to the McMichaels then headed down the street toward his mobile unit.

"Looks like everything's fine," my mom said. "Let's give thanks for that. The last thing Poly needs is to get involved in another murder investigation."

I barely heard the ribbing that took place at my expense. I should have been happy that the mystery was solved, that Mr. Estabrook was alive and well and preparing to share a Thanksgiving meal with his wife. But it wasn't like me to jump to conclusions, not like this. My mom wasn't wrong; I'd been involved in more than one murder investigation since moving to San Ladrón, one of them even involving my family. But I didn't suspect everyone I met of being a criminal. That wasn't who I was. Was it? Had I lost my ability to meet people and get to know them without assuming the worst?

While I kept the binoculars trained on the window, I watched Vaughn and his dad talk to each other. Vaughn pointed at my windows, and his dad shook his head. A tiny part of me regretted not making Vaughn's dad feel more welcome while he was here. He'd been nothing but cordial despite the passively hostile environment. I didn't blame him for not wanting to return.

The two men hugged, then Mr. McMichael crossed the street and climbed into his silver BMW. Vaughn looked both ways and went back inside the bar. The BMW pulled away from the curb. A few seconds later, the door reopened, and Duke rolled himself out. The man in the purple sweater followed. Duke pointed up and down the street and then shook his head. There was no familiarity between them, nothing to suggest they'd ever met before.

There was no way, simply *no way* Duke would not recognize his tenant!

I lowered the binoculars. "I'll admit a man went into Duke's bar," I said, "but it was *not* Mr. Estabrook."

"Poly," my mom admonished, her annoyance with me evident in her tone. "Genevieve made a great effort to cook you a delightful Thanksgiving meal. You're surrounded by friends and family. If you can't find a way to relax and enjoy this day, then we're going to leave after dessert."

My mom and I had a stare-off. She was right. My apartment smelled wonderful all day thanks to Genevieve, first her orange clove muffins and blueberry buckle, then tea, then the savory scent of rosemary-rubbed turkey, buttery potatoes, and pumpkin bisque. Now it was coffee and pie, cloves and ginger and cinnamon and more pumpkin, apple pie for the contingency who wanted something different, and Tangorli meringue, because Tangorlis—a tangerine-orange-lime hybrid—were unique to San Ladrón. Genevieve wanted to make today special and create a pie to honor the small hometown that brought us together. It was all courtesy of my friend, not Little Tony's Ristorante, with its white napkins and gold utensils, not the historic Waverly House with its award-winning chef, not Earl of Sandwich, with their lean meats and budget prices. And my mom was right. They were *all* right. I'd been so focused on convincing the rest of them that something bad had happened across the street that I didn't stop to see all the good that was happening right here.

I set the binoculars on the window ledge. "Fine," I said. "I'm done with the Estabrooks."

The tension in the room hung for a moment, as if cheesecloth had been suspended over the room, all parties collectively holding their breath waiting for me to say *just kidding* or *never mind* or add *after today*. When I didn't, the energy shifted. My mom even tipped her head and assessed my hair. "That style looks good on you."

One by one my mom, dad, Big Joe, Maria, and the boys collected in the kitchen to select their choice of dessert. My dad helped me up and guided me to the dining room. The gate sounded downstairs, and a few seconds later, Vaughn burst through the doorway.

"Hey, Vaughn," Big Joe said. "You're just in time for pie."

I caught Vaughn's eye from across the table. His brows were slightly drawn. He had something on his mind, but whatever it was, he didn't share it with the group.

One by one, Genevieve distributed plates of pie. Carlos took a slice of all three, and Antonio took a plate of fresh whipped cream with a side of pumpkin pie. As the hostess, I waited until last to make my request, watching the pumpkin pie (my choice) disappear.

I declined the last slice of Tangorli meringue. "Thank you for making us a great meal," I said to Genevieve when she topped off my tea. "You've outdone yourself."

She smiled sweetly. "I've never had a chance to plan and execute my dream Thanksgiving meal before. Today was almost perfect."

I smiled back, aware that the "almost" was thanks to me.

Genevieve carried a cup of lilac tea sweetened with local honey to the table and sat. Conversation fell silent, replaced by the clink of forks against plates and spoons swirling the contents of mugs. It was pleasant, relaxing even, to push my suspicions to the back of my mind and savor the tang of the pie and let the toasted meringue dissolve against the tip of my tongue. The table setting was a mismatch of china and fabric and flowers picked from the gardens around us, and it looked as it might have looked fifty years ago when my relatives hosted Thanksgiving at this very same table before half of us had been born.

Between bites, I turned to my parents. "I've been trying to find a buyer for some of the older fabrics in my inventory. Chiffon, radzimir, lace, tulle. They're the slowest sellers that I have, and I need space to expand other categories."

"You can think about that tomorrow, Poly," my mom said. "It's Thanksgiving. Let your father enjoy a dessert that doesn't say Little Debbie on the box."

My dad didn't have a comeback, largely because his mouth was full of pie. "I know, I know. It's just—I'm busy all day, and by the time the shop is closed, I collapse into bed. I thought I could use today to finish up with inventory so I would know what I could sell, but now this ankle is going to make my job that much more difficult." I poked at my pie with the times of my fork.

"You need to slow down. You're in such a hurry to get this place up and running that you forgot why you reopened it in the first place. Your aunt and uncle bought those fabrics. They represent the journey this store made from when it just a dream to what it is today under your ownership."

The gate to my shop slammed open and, judging from the sound of the boots clomping up the stairs, Charlie was back. As was her nature, she burst through the entranceway.

"Yo, Big Joe. Your fan belt's fixed. You can take off whenever you want." She tossed a set of keys to him, which he caught in his left hand while holding his fork in the right. He glanced at Maria, who shifted her eyes to the boys.

"After pie," she said. "I'm sure the boys will be hungry again in an hour."

Genevieve looked at me. "There's a second pumpkin pie in the oven. You'll have to wait about thirty minutes until it's out and cooled enough to eat."

"Is there coffee?" I asked.

"I'll join you," Vaughn said. I appreciated the offer of company, but I couldn't help thinking there was something he wanted to share about the happenings across the street. I didn't break my word, but I didn't announce a moratorium on observing suspicious behavior either.

Vaughn, who had no way of knowing what had transpired while he was gone, helped me back into the living room. He glanced at the telescope and the binoculars then sat in the Queen Anne chair. "Why is the place is so quiet? What did I miss?"

"People are not on board with my suspicions about the Estabrooks. After we saw him go back inside, they ganged up on me."

Vaughn grinned. “Your mother?”

“Yep.”

I fought the urge to resume my surveillance. Now that I’d agreed to enjoy the day, it seemed wrong to go back on my word at the first opportunity.

“Once I said I was done with the Estabrooks, they relaxed. Between the tryptophan, the carbs, and the pie, my parents should be napping on the sofa by now.”

“I heard that!” my dad called out.

If he heard that, then I had to be careful. I lowered my voice. “It seems my theories about the goings-on in the apartment over Duke’s bar are not appropriate for Thanksgiving. You believed me. They don’t, but you do—or you did. Do you still?”

Vaughn rubbed his eyes. “I want to believe you. You’re not a sky-is-falling type, and if you say you heard something suspicious, I think you heard something suspicious. But it’s hard to argue with the fact that Mr. Estabrook, the person you think was the victim of a violent crime, just went back to his apartment with no signs of injury.”

He had a good point. I sipped my coffee, not exerting any more energy on the Estabrooks. Genevieve carried a plate of Tangorli meringue pie into the room, and Charlie followed her.

Genevieve took a much-earned rest on the sofa, and Charlie, who did not know the telescope was to be avoided at all costs, peered through it at the apartment across the street.

"Huh," she said. "What's he doing over there?"

"Mr. Estabrook came home while you were fixing Big Joe's car," Genevieve said from behind her. "Poly admitted she was wrong, and now we're finally enjoying Thanksgiving."

"That's not Mr. Estabrook," Charlie said. "That's the guy who came over to check out Poly's fabric."

14

"IT'S WHO?" I ASKED. I REACHED OUT TO SWING THE telescope toward me, but Charlie kept her hand on it.

"The guy in the purple sweater. He was here earlier. Remember when you asked me to go downstairs and do you a favor? And I did? And you lacked the proper appreciation?"

"How could I forget?" I asked though that wasn't the important question. "But that doesn't make sense. Why would my prospective fabric buyer go to the Estabrooks?"

"Maybe he had other appointments in town. I admit it's a weird day to go door-to-door."

While Charlie spoke, Vaughn pulled the binoculars out of their case and looked back across the street. Genevieve abandoned her pie and joined us. She pushed

Charlie aside and peered through the telescope. "Is that my muffin basket?"

Without access to the binoculars or telescope, I couldn't see much through the windows across the street, but I recognized the colorful wicker basket Charlie and I had carried over earlier this morning in our role as welcome wagon. It sat on the kitchen counter and blocked my view of the table.

Genevieve pulled out her phone and pressed a button. Whoever she tried to call didn't answer.

"Didn't Duke go home?" she asked Vaughn after disconnecting.

Vaughn nodded. "He's downstairs in his office. Said he had some paperwork to finish."

I took the binoculars from Vaughn's hands and looked across the street. Two people were moving around the apartment above Duke's bar: a man and a woman. In the bedroom, a trunk was open on the bed. The man in the purple sweater packed the trunk. The last thing he did was pull the purple sweater off and shove it inside. He closed the trunk and secured it with rope. I looked back through the windows that showed the kitchen where the woman—Mrs. Estabrook?—stood with her phone pressed to her head. The taper candles had burned down since she first lit them. If I strained my eyes, I could make out the bright-orange indicator light on her oven. The scene didn't match the setting.

These looked like two people who planned to leave town, not two people preparing to sit down for a romantic meal and give thanks for having a roof over their heads.

"Poly!" My mom's voice rang sharply through the living room like a crack from a shotgun. When I looked at her, her stare burned through me. I pointed at the window. "It's not what you think."

She turned back to my dad. "John, what do you say we go downstairs and check out what Poly's done with the fabric store before we head home?"

"Mom, you guys don't have to leave."

"Oh, Poly, I think we do. John?"

"Sure," my dad said. He didn't look as disappointed in me as my mom did, but Genevieve's pie may have softened him.

"Maria, go get the boys," Big Joe said. "We should be heading out too."

My mom and dad waved to me from the doorway. "Go to the doctor tomorrow. Have that ankle looked at."

"It's just a sprain," I protested for what felt like the fifteenth time.

I watched as Big Joe, Maria, Carlos, Antonio, and my parents left. I listened as the footsteps descended the staircase and the gate retracted. My parents had parked in the lot behind the shop, so I shifted my attention to the window and watched the Lopezes climb into the donut delivery van Charlie had parked in front. Seconds later, they drove away.

Of the four of us left, three were on board the suspicious behavior theory. Genevieve had been in the kitchen for most of the day, and in the few minutes she'd spent out here, she'd sided with my parents. I knew she had been looking forward to cooking Thanksgiving for us but also to spending time with Duke, who left after too many implications that in his haste to collect rent money, he'd leased his renovated apartment to a murderer. If I could get up and walk, I would have gone across the street myself, apologized, and dragged Duke back. The irony was that here I was in Duke's loaner wheelchair. I was as trapped here as he was there.

Oh no.

Thoughts tend to come at us not always like bullets, but like clouds, faint at first, then taking shape. As the thought blossoms, it brings with it meaning. The edges of the thought bleed into other thoughts that maybe wouldn't normally connect, implications that set off warning flares about what might come next if ignored. That's how it felt when I thought of Duke, alone, in his apartment across the street.

Duke, who had a file on the two people who rented out the apartment overhead.

Duke, who resisted my theories, but may very well have stayed behind to check things out on his own. And if he'd found something, he might have wanted to deal with them himself.

I turned to Vaughn. "How was Duke when you left him?"

"He was tired. He said he wanted to finish with some paperwork, then he was going to take a nap. Why?"

It was Genevieve who answered Vaughn's question. "Because if Poly's right about the Estabrook's not being who they say they are, he might be in trouble."

15

VAUGHN WAS QUICK TO STAND. "I'LL GO CHECK ON HIM."

"Wait," Genevieve said. We all looked at her. She chewed her bottom lip nervously, then, as if landing on one side of an internal debate, nodded. "I'm coming with you."

"Genevieve—" I protested.

She untied her apron and tossed it onto the sofa. "I bought that basket at a vintage market in Lyon," she said, pointing at the window. "I want it back."

No matter how big a memento that basket was, I didn't believe for a second the reason Genevieve was going with Vaughn was to retrieve it. All morning she'd pooh-poohed my suspicions, but now she must have realized there was a note of—if not truth, then possibility—to what I said. That it wasn't all the result of a sleep-deprived imagination. She was showing a brave face because she cared about Duke, probably more than she'd admit to any of us, but she was also the one person here who thought I might be wrong.

I put my hand on Vaughn's hand and curled my fingers around his. His hand was warm from his cup of coffee, and his palm was smooth, the result of having a desk job, and not rough with calluses like mine were from working in the fabric shop. I stared into his eyes, and he stared back. I couldn't go across the street with him, not with this swollen ankle. I'd be more of a hindrance than a help.

"Be careful," I said.

"I'm coming with," Charlie said. She glanced at me. "Poly doesn't need me here, and somebody has to keep an eye on Frenchie."

In the span of eight hours, I went from waking up alone, to having a one-bedroom apartment filled with twelve people, and now, it was back to just me. As if on cue, Pins and Needles slinked into the living room. Pins hopped up on the sofa across the room, and Needles jumped on the coffee table and licked the plate where Genevieve had left a now-melting puddle of whipped cream.

"You believe me, don't you?" I asked. Pins raised his head and meowed while Needles licked his paw and swiped his head. I'd take that as a yes.

Left alone, there was nothing to keep me from watching what happened across the street. The binoculars were closer to me than the telescope, so I picked them up and watched my closest friends enter the Broadside. The heavy wooden door swung closed, and I lost sight of them after that.

Before I'd tuned into the suspicious activity in the apartment across the street, I took note of Tina at her salon and Earl in his apartment. I moved the binoculars to each of their apartments, but between the darkness brought on by the rainstorm and now, the sun setting behind the buildings, it was impossible to see inside. Each of their windows were dark, shades drawn.

I shifted my attention back to the Estabrooks. Mrs. Estabrook approached the door and opened it. Charlie and Genevieve entered. Gen pointed at the muffin basket, and Mrs. Estabrook nodded and smiled. She pointed at the oven then over her shoulder toward what I knew was the bedroom.

The three women appeared to chat, and then Genevieve and Charlie left. The basket remained behind. Mrs. Estabrook stood with her ear pressed against it after they were gone. Satisfied that they'd left, she went back to the counter and picked up the muffin basket. I watched as she flipped the plaid fabric open and peered inside. The human thing to do would be to take a muffin, or maybe to cover the muffins back up and add them to her oversized handbag. Even a criminal needs a snack on the road. But anger rose as I watched her pick up the basket and shove it into her oven. She spun the temperature dial.

The candles were still burning. The oven light was still on. There was no movement in the apartment over Duke's bar, but four people I cared about—Genevieve, Charlie, Vaughn, and Duke—had been there moments ago. Four people who could be anywhere: trapped inside or asleep thanks to a gas leak. If that oven was on and Genevieve's muffin basket was inside, it was just a matter of time until the contents caught fire and the apartment went up in flames, taking people I cared deeply about along with it.

I shifted my focus from the kitchen to the bedroom.

Mrs. Estabrook was standing by the windows looking back at me.

16

I DROPPED INTO THE WHEELCHAIR AND WHEELED IT backward. The chair connected with the telescope stand, and I knocked it over. I tried to maneuver the chair around it and failed. The wheels were blocked by the thin wooden stilt of the telescope stand.

I scanned the room for my cell phone. It was on the coffee table. I pushed myself out of the wheelchair and bent my knee to keep weight off my ankle. The door opened downstairs. Relief flooded me.

"Call Sheriff Clark!" I called.

But the person who entered the fabric store didn't sound like they were making a phone call to the local sheriff's mobile unit. Footsteps sounded on the wooden stairs that led to my apartment over the store, slow and steady footsteps, getting closer. I turned around to look at the windows, but I was too far away from them to make out the details of movement with my naked eyes.

The footsteps reached my landing. I couldn't know if whoever was there knew where I was in the apartment, but the fact remained, I was up here, unable to leave thanks to a sprained ankle and a lack of exits on this level. If I had any chance to get out, it lay in a surprise attack.

I tested my ankle. Pain. I put my hand on the coffee table to bear a portion of my weight. Mrs. Estabrook came through my dining room and blocked my exit.

Adrenaline coursed through me, and I stood to my full height. The flouncy white chiffon of my dress skirt exposed my thick, batting-wrapped ankle, but I was on the other side of the coffee table, and Mrs. Estabrook couldn't see that. She couldn't know the wheelchair was for me and not Duke.

I inched the chair closer to her. I had one way out, and it was through her.

"What did you do with him?" I asked.

She leveled her gaze at me. "Why do you care?"

She didn't deny my implication.

She didn't ask who.

"You murdered your husband," I accused. I inched my way around the coffee table. "You murdered your husband and you rolled his body up in your carpet." For the first time that day, I heard how crazy I must have sounded to everybody who had been here at some point of the day, but there was no going back now. "You arranged to have the rolled-up rug carried out of your apartment and delivered to the one being renovated down the street. How did you know?"

Mrs. Estabrook came deeper the room. She advanced around the coffee table. I inched my way back, staying on the opposite side, trying not to favor my ankle and let her know my mobility was compromised.

"Every business on this street is closed for Thanksgiving. One week in this sleepy town was more than enough to learn everybody's plans. You should have paid attention to your party of orphans instead of snooping on mine. It's sad to be alone on the holidays, isn't it? That won't be a problem for you next year."

She came closer. If I rushed her, I'd lose. My ankle couldn't handle a charge attack. But she had no weapon. No gun aimed at me. I didn't have much of a plan, just that I had to get around the table and through the kitchen. I didn't know how to slow her down. Once I stepped away from the coffee table, she'd see my batting-wrapped ankle and know I wasn't much of a threat.

Except I was. I was the one person who saw her movements all day long. My post by the window had made me an expert witness. I knew she left during the storm. I knew she had two men carry a carpet from her apartment. I knew she had an accomplice in the form of the man in the purple sweater, the same man who had come to my fabric store to examine my fabric.

That visit was never about making an offer on my fabric. It was about distraction. People had been coming and going from my place all day, and that made us the most likely threat to whatever crime it was she and her partner had planned to commit.

I'd managed to make a full circle of the coffee table. If I didn't make a break for it now, she'd catch me. And now that she knew what I knew, she knew I was the one person who stood between her and freedom.

I stepped away from the coffee table. Mrs. Estabrook's eyes shifted down the length of my body, and she saw my ankle. Her features changed into something nearing a smile. She crept toward me, and I inched backward. I put my hands out for anything to help offset my weight.

"Two cripples in one town? It's like I hit the lottery."

Rage spread through me. She closed the gap between us, and I raised my arms to defend myself, my hands landing on her shoulders to keep her from grabbing me. She moved forward, and I was no match for her force. I stumbled through the kitchen, past the second pumpkin pie cooling on Genevieve's baker's rack, past the stack of dirty dishes in the sink, past the apron Mr. McMichael wore while helping to chop vegetables. I felt tears, hot and searing, burning my eyes and falling down my face as I struggled through the pain, but I was no match for a woman motivated by hate and fear. She wrestled me backward to the landing above my stairs then shared the goal I'd had, to get me down the stairs, but not slow and steady like I would have liked. She forced my hands off her shoulders and pushed, and I tumbled, ass over teakettle, in a blur of sheer white chiffon and blinding pain, until the pile of fabrics I'd left stacked at the bottom of the stairs broke my fall.

The last thing I thought before I passed out was, "So *that's* what a broken ankle feels like."

17

A WEEK LATER, I RETURNED TO MY LIVING ROOM. DUKE was in my kitchen helping Genevieve remake her Thanksgiving meal. Charlie was in the Queen Anne chair, across from Clark, playing their fifth game of backgammon. Big Joe and Maria Lopez were on the sofa. Carlos knelt on the floor, dangling a piece of yarn over Needles's head. The last I'd heard, Antonio was downstairs in the fabric store with Pins. My mom and dad were down there, too, deciding which bolts of fabric they wanted to take back home with them to give me space for my fabric shop expansion.

My ankle was in a cast, broken in two places. Quite possibly the only thing that kept me from breaking more bones than that was the pile of sheer fabrics that had been stacked by the bottom of the stairs with the intent to sell. Maybe I'd been presumptuous.

Mrs. Frances Estabrook was behind bars awaiting trial for the murder of her husband. She might have gotten away with it, too, if Charlie and I hadn't gone over with a basket of muffins to welcome her to the neighborhood. What I didn't know at the time was that Charlie had completed the task of leaving a note. It wasn't the gesture that made all the difference, it was what she wrote: *We saw you from across the street.*

When a woman murders her husband and then has his body rolled up in a gravy-stained carpet and removed from her newly rented apartment then receives a muffin basket with that note, well, it doesn't really matter what comes after that line, does it? Charlie claims it was something pithy—*happy thanksgiving from the neighborhood welcome wagon*—but knowing Charlie, I seriously doubted her message was all sweet and innocent. Whatever she wrote, it was gone, burned up in the fire that stemmed from Genevieve's muffin basket being shoved into a five-hundred-degree oven and left to incinerate and burn the place down.

Causing a diversion for local law enforcement while tangentially destroying any evidence. No dummy, that Mrs. Estabrook. She seemed to have thought of everything, if not a little too late.

When she spotted me watching her, she wove

together frayed edges of the perceived threat of being caught. She left out the back windows, down the fire escape—a bit of irony there—and across the street where my gate was open thanks to the flow of guests coming and going all day. And after she confronted me, while we did our slow dance around the coffee table, my friends had been busy. They took turns sharing the details while I recovered.

Duke, it turned out, hadn't just gone home to watch the game. He pulled the file on the Estabrooks and checked their rental application. Even though it was a holiday, he was able to find out in the span of two phone calls that they weren't who they claimed to be. By the time my friends showed up to tell him to get out of there, he knew I'd been right.

From there, they divided and conquered.

Vaughn went upstairs to check on the Estabrooks. When he touched the doorknob, it was hot. Smoke trickled from under the door. He'd raced downstairs for the fire extinguisher Duke kept behind the bar and busted down the door while Charlie ran up a red flag for Clark and the fire department.

Duke went for his prized shotgun.

I would have liked to see the look on Mrs. Estabrook's face as she stood on my landing, watching me fall down the stairs, thinking her problems were solved, only to be met with her landlord in his wheelchair sighting her through his gun scope. I guess there's more than one way to spy on your neighbor.

My recovery hadn't been a solo affair. Vaughn moved in for the week, catering to my every need. My parents said it was a trial run. Charlie said it was about time. I said they all needed to mind their own business.

But today, one week after it all went down, I had a full house. Genevieve was in the kitchen slicing a freshly baked pumpkin pie. She carried a tray into the living room and distributed plates and forks. She started with Duke and Charlie, and I was a little worried I wasn't going to get any pie this time either when she stopped in front of me and handed me a serving.

My "slice" was a quarter of the pie. It was a good thing I had nothing else on my plate so I could relax and enjoy it.

EXCERPT: CONTESTING THE WOOL

Keep reading for a sneak peek at CONTESTING THE WOOL, the next Material Witness mystery!

1

THE READING OF REGINALD VILLAMERE'S WILL WAS THE event of the season, and until last week, I didn't know the man existed. That was the day the official invitation requesting my presence at the private ceremony was delivered to Material Girl, the fabric shop I had inherited. The return address on the envelope was McMichael Investments. Vaughn and I had been dating over the past several months, and I assumed the invitation was a perk of being his girlfriend.

That didn't mean I wasn't going to go.

I hadn't had a chance to ask Vaughn about the invitation, but aside from my curiosity about his willingness to trade on his firm's reputation to get me a seat to San Ladrón's latest roadside attraction, the answers to any questions I had about the agenda were contained within the letter. The reading of the will was scheduled to take place in the conference room of the Villamere, our small town's historic-yet-neglected theater, and Reginald Villamere's legal team would be in attendance to oversee the proceedings. Confidentiality was requested, and I had a feeling "requested" was a misleading choice of words. Phrases like "legal team" suggested there would be signed and notarized documents involved. Vaughn and I had been getting closer of late, but an entrée to the reading was a step beyond my recent offer to provide the fabric to reupholster his new sofa.

I parked my VW Bug in the Villamere parking lot, grabbed my handbag, and dug around on the passenger-side floor for my cane. Last Thanksgiving I'd broken my ankle after an unfortunate tumble down the stairs that led to the shop below my apartment. Klutzy was my middle name, but in that case, there'd been a life-and-death situation that took priority over a calm and orderly descent down the stairs. My broken ankle was a small price to pay. The injury would have healed by now on a person who'd never had an ankle injury before, but I'd been accident-prone my whole life, and sad to say, injury recovery now took more time. The orthopedic team advised me that if I rushed my rehab, I'd be looking at pain for the rest of my life. That didn't sound like a winning gamble, so a cane it was.

A man in an expensive gray flannel suit held the door of the theater open for me. I picked up my pace so as not to inconvenience him, though there was a good chance we were headed to the same place. I thanked him and entered the building, then I stood off to the side of the lobby. I was rooting around in my bag for my letter of invitation when I heard Vaughn call my name.

"Poly?"

It took a moment to spot his location. The Villamere lobby had been renovated sometime in the eighties, expanding the original concession area to include high-top tables and a bar. The theater itself had been built in the thirties, and renovations since then had honored the original concept but not for some time. Carpets were worn where foot traffic was high, faded in spots and stained in others. There were two screens for projecting classic movies and two stages for hosting live performances, though both showed signs of water damage after heavy flooding seeped through an already damaged ceiling.

The theater was not without some upgrades. Some time since the theater's opening, a landing had been added to the floor plan, and now exhibits of movie memorabilia were regularly on display. As many times as I'd come here to enjoy an old movie being projected onto a big silver screen, I'd never once thought about the fact that there was a real live member of the Villamere family who owned the place. Considering I was here for a reading of his will, I guess there wasn't anymore.

I scanned the lobby then looked up a long circular staircase that ran up the center of the building to the second-floor landing. That was when I spotted Vaughn jogging down the stairs toward me. It would take him less time to descend the stairs than it would for me to climb them, so I tucked my invitation back into my handbag and waited patiently for him to reach the bottom step.

"What are you doing here?" he asked.

"Ha, ha," I said. "Did you really think I was going to miss this?"

Vaughn looked embarrassed. "I didn't think you'd crash it."

At this, I stepped back and studied Vaughn's expression. He looked cautiously nervous, and I knew he wasn't kidding. "I'm not crashing it. I got your invitation. I assumed it was a perk of dating you."

Vaughn raised his eyebrows. "A perk?"

"You know what I mean."

"I think you've been spending too much time with my sister."

Instead of debating that possibility, I pulled the invitation out of my handbag and extended the thick, creamy envelope toward him. "Did you not send me this?"

He accepted the envelope and slid the invitation out,

then he scanned the text. Unless someone had gone to great lengths to prank me, the invitation was legitimate. Vaughn ran his thumb over the raised logo and return address on his dad's company's letterhead and reread the contents. Eventually, he looked up and held the letter back out to me.

"I didn't send you this."

"But it's legit, right? I didn't misinterpret it?"

"One of our new interns must have made a mistake. I'll talk to them on Monday. As long as you're here, you might as well come in and observe."

Vaughn turned away from me and started up the staircase. I remained rooted in place. He turned back. "Are you coming? Do you need help getting up the stairs?"

"As fun as it sounds to get to sit in on the reading of Villamere's will, if it's going to be a problem for you, I'll go home. I don't want to get anybody in trouble."

Vaughn retraced his steps. "The lawyers are going to have a list of everyone who received an invitation. They won't start the proceedings until all are present. At this point, it'll create more of a problem if you don't come than if you do." He crooked his arm and offered me his elbow. "This place should have put in an elevator by now, but plans always got hung up by the historical preservation people. The conference room is on the second floor. Can you make it?"

"Just try to stop me."

Climbing the stairs took longer than I would have liked, but I made it up the winding staircase and followed Vaughn past the landing to a small hallway. Another man, this one in a brown wool suit with a navy windowpane pattern, stood outside a propped-open door. He had white AirPods in his ears, and he appeared to be embroiled in a heated discussion with the person on the other end of a call. He walked back and forth in the small hallway, gesturing wildly even though the person on the other end of his call couldn't see him.

"There's nothing I can do about it until we locate her," he said. "Until then, my hands are tied."

The good thing about using a cane is that people expect you to move slowly, and I took full advantage of that expectation on my way to the door. The man was on a "forth" leg of his back-and-forth, which gave me a few seconds to study him. Broad shoulders, narrow waist. A full head of thick, steely hair cut into a neat style. Double vented jacket. Fancy watch. Broadcloth shirt. Piercing blue eyes.

Uh-oh. He'd turned around and caught me staring at him.

I smiled, hoping cute and friendly with a cane was a winning—or at least auspicious—combination. The man scanned me, auburn hair to moto boots and back up to my face, and returned to his call.

I entered the conference room. Chairs had been set up in classroom formation facing a long table covered in leather binders and weighty writing instruments. I propped my cane under a vacant seat in the back row and hung the oversized black blazer, the one I'd taken out of my great-uncle's side of the closet, over the back of the chair. He and my great-aunt had left me the fabric store and the apartment above it, including the contents, and the contents included their wardrobes.

Despite the numerous options available at the concession stand on the first floor, a pink bakery box with the Lopez Donuts logo sat on a table at the back of the room. I headed toward the table and helped myself to a cruller. When I turned, I caught Vaughn watching me. He stifled a smile.

The man from the hallway entered the room and cleared his throat. "People, please take your seats. We'll get started at the top of the hour." He glanced at his watch, and most people glanced at their phones.

I checked the clock on the wall. The second hand swept from the five, traced around the bottom quadrant of the clock, and closed in on the twelve just as the minute hand did the same.

Vaughn took his seat at the table at the front of the room, next to the gray-haired man. The man from the parking lot in the expensive wool suit sat at the end of the table and opened a leather folio. As the proceedings started, he took notes. His left hand curled around his marbled pen, leaving behind slashes of ink on a formerly neat document. I wondered whether someone back at the office was going to have to decipher that, or whether workplace standards had changed and he'd do it himself.

I smoothed my black skirt over my black tights and silenced my phone. Now that I knew I was here by accident, it made sense to draw as little attention to myself as possible. I was inquisitive by nature and had more than a passing interest in things from the thirties, so Vaughn's intern's error was appreciated. Even though I would be bound by the confidentiality agreement that was attached to these proceedings, I was curious about who would get what. San Ladrón was a town of secrets, I'd discovered in the short time since I'd inherited the fabric shop and moved into the Victorian apartment above it, and even though I wouldn't discuss what I learned today with anybody other than Vaughn, I had a feeling the knowledge might come in handy.

Hollywood portrays will readings as exciting events filled with greedy employees and backstabbing relatives. If that was the case here, then people were on their best behavior. In addition to the lawyer who seemed to be in charge, there was a middle-aged white couple in the front row, a cluster of theater employees in burgundy Villamere uniforms in the second, and an older woman with a chic gray bob in an ivory pantsuit on the other end of the back row with me. More of the chairs were vacant than not. The so-called "event of the season" was sparsely populated.

Vaughn closed the door to the conference room and returned to the table. He nodded at the gray-haired man, and the proceedings started.

"I'm Ben Schaffley of Schaffley, Bozer, and Schmidt," he said. "We represent the estate of Reginald Villamere. Mr. Vaughn McMichael is here as a representative of McMichael Investments acting as the executor of the will. In the event someone contests the will, my team will act as an intermediary with Mr. McMichael's office to reach a resolution. It should be noted that the will in question has been on file for over thirty years. Mr. Villamere did not respond to regular requests to update the document. Because of the lapsed time, there exists the possibility that surviving relatives of named inheritors will have to be found and notified."

Murmurs made their way around the room. The world had changed significantly since the will had been written, and who knew what Reginald Villamere had thought at the time.

"The first item on file is the collection of textiles left after the most recent renovation of the Villamere Theater was completed. Any and all materials are hereby bequeathed to the owners of Land of a Thousand

Fabrics." The lawyer looked up. "Are Marius or Millie Monroe present?"

My throat hitched. Marius and Millie were not present, but their heir was. I slowly raised my hand. It turned out my invitation wasn't an intern's mistake after all.

ACKNOWLEDGMENTS

Early in 2024, a fellow author approached me about writing a Thanksgiving-themed novella. I already had a few projects on my slate, but I couldn't shake the idea. Would this feature Samantha Kidd? Madison Night? Would I discover what Thanksgiving meant in outer space? I rotated through a few ideas, none quite fitting, until I realized one set of my characters hadn't gotten a story this year. So, I was headed back to San Ladrón.

It's always been in the back of my mind to do a story inspired by *Rear Window*, and this felt the time. It took me one interactive Facebook post to determine that *Radzimir Window* was not a good title, but Lisa Q. Mathews stepped up with *Sheer Window* and from there, the rest fell into place—until it fell out of place and my writing support group stepped in to ask me: why are you writing a *Rear Window* story that isn't a *Rear Window* story? Back to the drawing board I went!

So, my biggest thank you goes out to my author friends: Lisa Q. Mathews, Ellen Byron, and Gigi Pandian, for not letting me veer too far off the path, and Julie

Mulhern for suggesting the project in the first place. Thank you to my readers, who kept Poly alive and well for years before she returned in *Tulle Death Do Us Part,* and are there for her turn as Thanksgiving host. Thank you to Alfred Hitchcock, to whom this novella is dedicated, for the inspiration, to Grace Kelly for wearing *that dress*, and to Edith Head for making it in the first place.

Thanks to Red Adept Editing and to the Polyester Posse for your ongoing support, and to my Weekly DiVa club members, for coming along with me on this journey.

Happy Thanksgiving!

Xo,

Diane

ABOUT THE AUTHOR

National bestselling author Diane Vallere writes funny, and fashionable character-based mysteries. After two decades working for a top luxury retailer, she traded fashion accessories for accessories to murder. A past president of Sisters in Crime, Diane started her own detective agency at age ten and has maintained a passion for shoes, clues, and clothes ever since. Find out more at dianevallere.com.

ALSO BY

<u>Killer Fashion Mysteries</u>

Designer Dirty Laundry

Buyer, Beware

The Brim Reaper

Some Like It Haute

Grand Theft Retro

Pearls Gone Wild

Cement Stilettos

Panty Raid

Union Jacked

Slay Ride

Tough Luxe

Fahrenheit 501

Stark Raving Mod

Gilt Trip

Ranch Dressing

Murder Italian Style

<u>Madison Night Mad for Mod Mysteries</u>

“Midnight Ice” (prequel novella)

Pillow Stalk

That Touch of Ink

With Vics You Get Eggroll

The Decorator Who Knew Too Much

The Pajama Frame

Lover Come Hack

Apprehend Me No Flowers

Teacher's Threat

The Kill of It All

Love Me or Grieve Me

Please Don't Push Up the Daisies

The Glass Bottom Hoax

<u>Sylvia Stryker Outer Space Mysteries</u>

Murder on a Moon Trek

Scandal on a Moon Trek

Hijacked on a Moon Trek

Framed on a Moon Trek

Warped on a Moon Trek

<u>Material Witness Mysteries</u>

Suede to Rest

Crushed Velvet

Silk Stalkings

Tulle Death Do Us Part

Sheer Window

Contesting the Wool

Costume Shop Mystery Series

A Disguise to Die For

Masking for Trouble

Dressed to Confess

Mermaid Mysteries

Dead in the Water

Non-Fiction

Bonbons for your Brain

DIANE VALLERE

where style meets sleuthing

or visit
dianevallere.com/books

www.ingramcontent.com/pod-product-compliance
Lightning Source LLC
Chambersburg PA
CBHW011141190726
48289CB00012B/3110
* 9 7 8 1 9 5 4 5 7 9 1 8 7 *